FORWARD

I didn't think about this very long.
I was told the first few lines I write will
make or break a manuscript. Keep it
short and simple, and tell the story.
The book is about what happens when
two most unlikely characters meet and
fall in love.
Imagination is the key that unlocks all
stories worth telling. Imagination keeps
us sane because we can escape into our
fantasies. Then is when a writer
records these dreams. When finished,
they become real if they weren't
already. It's up to the reader to believe.

DEDICATION

To Carolyn, my inspiration and my
dream.

On Wings of Peace

A Story of Love

I In the Beginning

1

Once upon a time there was a Seagull. His name was "Manny." Manny was a strong and healthy bird. He loved to fly high in the sky and be swept away into strong wind currents that carried him great distances over the open sea. He was a happy bird and enjoyed soaking in the sun and fishing. Many days Manny spent sitting on a piece of driftwood somewhere on a remote beach near the ocean feeling the salty blown mist on his face as waves crashed onto nearby rocks. He had a lot of seagull friends, but liked to fly by himself and express his freedom in solitude.

When we meet Manny he's a young and adventurous seagull, much larger than average, and endowed with a strong muscular body. Manny resembles the large west coast gulls more than the smaller and lighter east coast breed he came from. His wing span is so wide he not only can traverse long distances by air, but resembles a speeding falcon when flying high.

Manny is physically stunning and graceful. He's also a free spirit who loves to sway with the air tides atop a tropical palm. From the time Manny was a mere chick, he was different. He was never a weak bird. He always stood tall, even in the presence of adults. All of his friends admired him, because he wasn't simply a supreme specimen of "Gull-hood," he was as soft spoken as he was physically dominant. Manny always believed there was a special purpose to his life. He was fashioned for a reason, and must always be an example to his peers of the goodness and strength of "Gull-kind." Manny exuded energy, happiness, hope and love. He was kind to all and knew no enemies. At a very young age, Manny achieved a serenity most Gulls might pursue over a lifetime.

One sunny day, during an early morning flight, Manny witnessed something he had never seen. He was so high, and what was below seemed so small, he blinked in disbelief. Manny descended from his lofty course to take a closer look. As he drew closer, he focused on the most unbelievable sighting in his life.

There, perched on a rock was the most beautiful Mermaid he had ever imagined. As he circled he could clearly see her radiance. She was striking! Her golden fishtail glistened. Her scales were a glowing reflection wrapped around her waist. Her skin, from the waist up, was so fair it didn't have the appearance of ever being exposed to sun or salt. She appeared to be frail and strong at the same time. Her long golden hair was windblown and animated. Her eyes were a light blue-green and as transparent as clear pure water. Her lips full and smiling and her face glowing with a light that danced. She was the most beautiful creature he had ever seen. As soon as Manny laid eyes on her, he was in rapture.

Minnie was the name of the mermaid Manny was about to meet. Like Manny, she was an extraordinary creature amongst her species. Her posture was perfect and her smile was radiant. She was the most stunning mermaid ever created. Her striking features were much deeper than her scales. She was the absolute essence of innocence exposed only to the joy of living and happiness in her world.

Manny circled Minnie's little island in the middle of the sea. He circled from high, and for a very long time. With each circle he became a little braver and flew a little lower. He was nervous. Something was making his stomach turn. He thought he was getting dizzy. Finally, Manny gingerly landed on a rock with only a few feet of water between him and his soon to be new friend. From that short distance he could see her every detail, and savor the aroma of her sweet fishy fragrance. Manny was awe stricken and speechless for the first time in his life. His mind told him to make contact. To speak, flap his wings, and do something to turn her head. As he looked up from his feet after his perfect landing, he was startled. He didn't have to do anything. She was looking directly into his deep dark brown eyes. Immediately, she struck up a conversation. "I'm Minnie, what's your name Mr. Seagull?"

"I'm Manny. Hey that's cool. You're Minnie and I'm Manny. Sort of poetic eh?"

"Oh, I suppose. Maybe we have something in common. You're a bird and I 'm a fish, uh...sort of. I thought gulls hunted fish. Are you here to carry me off and feed me to your flock?" "Hardly Ma'am, I mean Minnie. I don't know how to say this. I'll do the best I can. I was out for my morning flight, and noticed the reflection of your golden scales from the water below. As I came in closer, I noticed your hair, your smooth skin and your beautiful transparent eyes. I wanted to meet you, and was feeling a bit woozy. Maybe I was flying too high, you know, lack of oxygen. Anyway, I landed here on this rock near you, and hoped you wouldn't thrash me with your tail. I only wanted to meet you. You're the most unusual sight I've seen this side of the ocean."

"Thanks Manny, that was flattering. First of all, I never thrash another creature with my tail except in self defense. I'm a Mermaiden. A peace loving half fish and half human creature who understands only feelings of love and peace in my heart. I swim the seas with my friends, and experience the vast wonders of our underwater universe. It's magnificent. Too bad you don't have gills. I'd take you on a tour that would knock your socks off! Have you ever seen a giant squid from the deep? Have you experienced what it is like to swim amongst living colorful coral? Every color you can possibly visualize and then some can be seen in these depths. I'm lucky because my human half allows me to take in the warmth of daylight above water, feel cool misty sea breezes and visualize so many unique wonders near the seashores. I'm amused how humans wear bright colors on the beaches. I call them human coral. Some of those colors are so bright and outrageous they really treat my eyes. I also get to see palm trees adding ambiance to the tropical landscape, and gigantic cruise ships making their way to and from port. Those we have to be careful of. They're so large, they can't see us smaller creatures, and we have to swim fast and deep to keep from being run over. Even though there is a lot of peril, such as fishing boats and the like, I am heartened by the colorful variety I see every day. Even in the deep, I have to stay alert, because of sharks and other sea predators, the likes of which you may have never seen. But, I will tell you this Manny, I always try to stay in a sunny world in my heart. Though I am aware of danger, I'm also aware of the rays of hope that inspire me and give me peace to carry on. When I sit here on these rocks, I see how calm the water is on the surface. It's a little like life you know. Sometimes I remind myself that just under the calm is chaos. Killer whales, sting rays and sharks might snatch me up in an instant while I'm enjoying the apparent calm ocean which is all I can see with my human eyes. I guess it makes sense though. Without warnings and dangers in life, how can I ever perceive opposites? Like everything else I guess there's a reason. Uh...Oh... Am I talking to much Manny? Tell me about your world...please?"

"Wow, Minnie. You are so eloquent and poetic. I've learned something here already. Maybe, it isn't the circumstances that surround us so much that make us who we are. Maybe it's all in what we make of them, how we see them and such. If all I want is to see pain and sadness, then that's what I'll see. If all I want to see are wonders of my mortal blessings, then that's what I'll see, even if the world surrounding me doesn't tell the same story. I am what I think. I am what I believe. I am who I let myself become. Thanks Minnie for opening my eyes. I suppose you want to hear about my seagull point of view?"

"Yes, I'd like to hear about what it's like to fly...and to see for miles. I want to know what you feel."

"Well, Minnie. I was born in a very different world than you. I never went very far under water, except when diving to catch a fish." I noticed a wincing expression. "Uh, I mean...well you know, a fella has to eat," I said with a restrained look. "Anyway," pause, "I've been blessed with strong wings and a strong body." I felt a little self-conscious then, and noticed Minnie was staring directly into my eyes. I swallowed, and continued. "My world has taken me many places. Tropical islands where there are majestic snow capped mountains, and steamy volcanoes. I've flown high in the sky and let the currents take me on fabulous journeys. I've seen breathtaking sites, and like you, I need to keep my eyes open for low flying airplanes and fishermen's nets when I am fishing. Every day's a new journey and a new experience. You should see the great painted birds I've met; toucans, parrots, and many varieties of canaries and bright colored finches.

However I will say this, in my travels I've never met anyone like you. Today is beyond anything I could imagine. I have no idea why, I just know it is."

The conversation between Manny and Minnie went on for hours. Both the young mermaid and seagull completely lost track of time. Manny apparently was attracted by Minnie's innocent smile, her golden tail, and long flowing hair. She projected radiance comparable to nothing Manny had ever envisioned. Minnie was in the same boat. She was attracted to Manny's kindness and demeanor, his strong and muscular countenance and those deep brown haunting eyes. Simply put, Manny and Minnie were completely taken with one another. Maybe it was love at first site.

Something else was happening. Manny and Minnie had forgotten who they were. Minnie was a mermaid, and Manny a seagull. What an unlikely combination. They were so different, but their new and budding friendship had transcended their most glaring differences. They only had one thing in common. They enjoyed each other's company. Isn't it interesting how the possibility of love can blossom anywhere? It doesn't matter where or who we are. When we can look beyond ourselves to see beauty in others and find love in the homeliest of all creatures, maybe we can begin to understand the phenomenal impact of this uncomplicated four letter word.

Now their first meeting was drawing to a close, and the sun was beginning to set in the west. The waters around Minnie roiled up like a submarine creating waves just before it surfaces. From below, a host of mermaids broke the surface. They swam around Minnie exhorting her to dive. It was time to go home. None of the mermaids noticed Manny sitting on the rock next to her. After all, he was only a bird, and of no consequence to them.

Minnie smiled as she looked deep into Manny's eyes.

"My new friend it's time to go. We have to dive very deep. It will be pitch dark by the time we get home, and I don't want to get lost. I always have a seaweed salad with the girls, and discuss our daily adventures. All I will talk about is you Manny. This has been a most wonderful day for me. Thank you for coming into my life, and laughingly I must say, you swooped down upon me and swept me right off my tail! I hope I will see you tomorrow."

"You will my lady, and all my friends will hear about you. I have to get back to the mainland. I've probably already missed dinner, because we hunt by light of day. I'll try to pick up some beach snacks left by tourists. And I must say to you, my majestic entrance into your life was more like a crash dive. I went completely limp at one point. It was when you looked up and saw me circling. As I looked into your eyes for the first time I almost forgot how to fly."

Manny smiled, then flew over and perched on Minnie's golden tail. She reached down and stroked his soft head with her gentle hands, then leaned over and kissed him lightly. Manny's dark eyes glistened in the setting sun as he looked deep into her transparent blue-green eyes. Manny smiled, "I will see you tomorrow, and this tender moment will be my memory." With that he departed into the heavens and disappeared over the horizon. Minnie watched until she could see him no more, then dove into the silent ocean and swam to her home under the sea.

2

"Seafaring locals" called their home the Crystal Cave. Most air-breathing deep sea creatures return there at sundown. This is where Minnie was born. It's located inside a gargantuan hollow mountain that rose up in the sea more than ten million years ago, and is adorned with many smaller caves full of stalagmites and stalactites which resemble fascinating monoliths, pillars and archways. In daylight the sun refracts through the depths and makes its way inward reflecting care free from its glistening walls to light every passage and pathway. At night the moon and stars emulate sunlight in a more subdued luminance. The cave is completely submerged in the ocean more than twenty-thousand leagues. It reaches to the center of the earth and rises near the surface on the other side. As water passes through almost sponge like perforated rock, air is filtered and released into main passageways which enrich Crystal Cave with sustenance of breathable pure oxygen. Herein is a delicate balance of nature that has survived many millennia. As sunrays penetrate the cave and water gives way to air, a ballet of light perpetually dances on the crystalline walls in tribute to the natural elements which create a living animated chorography.

Within the mammoth cave are smaller caves inhabited by countless families of exotic species living in peaceful harmony with each other. Mermaids and Manatees are the principal residents. Crystal Cave is often visited by dolphins and smaller air breathing whales as well. Also residing in this marine anomaly are an array of crustaceans, lobsters and funny looking little crabs. Water pools and eddies are nearly devoid of salt and many colorful freshwater fish live along side bright colored salt water fish and velvety pastel coral. Species of life never before seen, and some long thought extinct, reside in this paradise. Exotic hues radiate everywhere as a permanent color spectrum greets each new day with renewed brilliance.

Crystal Cave is the most unique place on earth. It is Eden underwater. No human has ever laid eyes on this treasure. No human ever will.

Crystal Cave is where Minnie was born. Like most newly born mermaids, Minnie was tiny, pale and frail. Her hair was thick, golden and curly. Her eyes sparkled like the reflections on the walls, and her smile melted everyone who looked in her crib. Minnie was the most beautiful mermaid ever born. She was special in so many ways. Minnie learned quickly and was extremely witty. Other mermaid children loved her infectious personality and zest for life.

Minnie was the brightest beacon in the Crystal Cave. All creatures who lived here, including those visiting, knew this little lady by name.

Minnie was a dreamer too. From the time she was very young she dreamed of adventures beyond her home. Her parents were patient with her, because Minnie was prone to daydream and sometimes missed her lessons in school. Somehow she made it through. Her interests and heart were always detached. Something out there was waiting for her to find. Minnie believed she was going to live all her dreams from childhood, and felt within herself she was embarking on an unusual adventure in her life ahead. Thoughts of Manny out there somewhere in a big and beautiful world made her smile and curl her lips upward in a Buddha half-smile that reflected her inner most thoughts as she strolled quietly through her heart of hearts.

Suddenly, she heard a LOUD splash, and a familiar song that made her smile.

"I'm Mattie the Man-a-tee...
I eat every- thing I see...
I travel near and far
to find a salad bar,
and have a little lunch.
Crunch. Crunch. Crunch, crunch, crunch.
I'm Mattie the Man-a-tee!"

As coincidence would have it, a young playful manatee next door possessed a similar name to Minnie's new seagull friend. Mattie was an interesting lad. All he wanted to do was eat and play.

Mattie loved everyone, trusted everyone, and lived life with abandon. His mother had been lost at sea, and his father taken by a boat propeller. Mattie was being raised by his grandparents, Floyd and Princess. Through all the tribulation Mattie experienced in his young life, he was able to find a poem in his heart, a smile to share and a song to sing.

The positive disposition of young Mattie could certainly be attributed to Floyd and Princess. Mostly Princess. Floyd was a wise and serious old Manatee. He knew the complete history of the Manatee blood line. A sea cow has a long memory because they are related to their land brothers the elephants. Old Floyd didn't say much, he observed everything. His very presence exuded vibrations of wisdom and contemplation.

Floyd knew where Mermaids came from and how they became such beautiful and gentle creatures. Princess, on the other hand, was a gregarious and outgoing Manatee. She was all about fun and social interaction. Floyd and Princess gave the best of both worlds to their little grandson Mattie. Mattie related more to fun and social interaction, and had an inner spirit which radiated a certain wise nature he was gradually acquiring from his ancient grandfather. Sometimes he sat for hours engrossed in the story telling of granddad, and then acted out in his play the magnificent roles Floyd painted with his paintbrushes of eloquent dialogue.

After dinner Minnie visited her girlfriends who were all gathered at the pool relaxing in the soft reflected moonlight.

As Minnie approached a small gathering of her sisters, all but two dove into the water giggling and laughing. Sara and Emily were the only two remaining at waters edge. They were her best friends.

"Hi ladies," said Minnie with a smile, "what's all the giggling about?"

"Oh," chimes in Sara, "just silly girl talk, that's all."

"Sure," as Emily clears her throat, "but maybe not so silly. I was in different waters today, and the girls told me you spent the entire day with an old smelly seagull. Is that true Minnie?"

Minnie took a deep breath, and spoke slowly, distinctly separating the first three words of her reply.

"Not...completely...true! I did spend the day with a seagull. He was neither old nor smelly. His name is Manny." Emily interrupted laughing. "Girl, you got too much sun today." Minnie scowled. "Let me finish! Manny is his name. Anyway, Manny the *SEAGULL* is about my age. If you would have seen him as I did, you might have noticed how extraordinary he is. Not just a strong and manly gull, but very clean, bright, worldly and sweet. He had the most beautiful big brown eyes you've ever seen. I enjoyed being with him. He was like a dream that just dropped out of the sky and almost landed in my lap. We're going to meet tomorrow too," she said curtly. "I think I really like him. I've never hoped for a day to end so much. I can't wait to be up there on the rocks tomorrow with Manny. Dad always said, don't wish for time to pass so quickly. Savor every day to its fullest, because once time passes that moment is gone and you are a little older but never closer to what you're looking forward to than if you live in the now. Tomorrow will come soon enough, maybe too soon. Don't wish your life away. Remember, today is all you have so cherish it. Well, he may be right, but I want tomorrow to be here as soon as possible so I can see my new friend Manny."

"Sounds more like new love than like to me," Sara said as she ran her hand through the shallow water alongside the pool.
Minnie didn't reply to either Emily or Sara again. She stood up, glanced their way with an impish grin, and leaned over to dive in the warm pool for a relaxing swim. After her dip, Minnie went home and crawled into her warm bed where sweet visions of Manny

flitted through her dreams throughout the night.

3

While Minnie was spending the evening with her family and friends, Manny was winging his way back to dry land. His home wasn't as elaborate as Minnie's. Since Manny left the nest, he lived in an old boot washed up on the beach long ago. It had floated past the tide line in a storm and wedged between two rocks on a very steep incline not accessible to humans and other animals. It was a perfect reclusive spot for Manny to rest and listen to the familiar sound of waves crashing into the rocks and washing upon the beach. His humble home was near a remote spot where a lot of tourists hung out and partied during the day. He often found a bit of human food somewhere left nearby. Manny lived this way because he didn't want to be burdened with the responsibility of maintaining a nest. He needed his freedom and open skies. Though the little home didn't rival the Crystal Cave, it was cozy and comfortable. The rocks wedging the shoe in place were positioned on a steep drop-off forming an upside down "V". On a warm night, Manny looked out over the ocean with an unobstructed view of every magnificent sunset. He had found a few old towel pieces and stuffed them in the boot to make a little nest where he looked out. If the weather was rainy or cold, Manny crawled to the open part of the "V" under the rocks where he enjoyed perfect shelter. In his little abode nestled in the rocks he had all the conveniences of home including an LCD high definition television, a microwave to heat leftovers, and a complete entertainment center with a booming stereo, video games and a high speed computer. Manny was a techno bird! On the outside, his place looked like a dump, but inside was a treasure trove of gadgets and store room for all the latest electronic technology including an electric tread mill and theater seats to watch football. The seats were equipped with a built in refrigerator for beer and snacks, and a humidor packed with savory Cuban Cigars. When Mr. Techno bird wanted to, he really enjoyed his stuff.

Manny had a flock of friends, and was often visited by the "boys." They played cards, argued about football and did things most young seagulls did. In the end, Manny appeared to be no different than every other gull on the beach. Upon closer examination, Manny was taller, more muscular, and when he flew he reached heights and speeds beyond the abilities of his peers. If seagull flying were an Olympic event, Manny owned the Gold!

It took over an hour for him to make his way home. Talk about hungry! He was ravenous by the time he made landfall. Manny was lucky that night. Some tourists had left an open cooler full of sandwiches and snacks. Manny dove in as if he were diving into deep water after a big juicy fish. Tuna Fish salad sandwiches were his absolute favorite, and he found three very thick and dripping sandwiches on top of melting ice. A one gull feeding frenzy was on.

Manny didn't stop until his belly was so full he looked pregnant. Full of food and having the best day of his life, Manny was tired but felt good. The night was warm and the moon so large it loomed like a giant pumpkin over a cerulean horizon.

It wasn't long before his buddies found him taking an evening walk along the coastline near his home. In seconds he was surrounded by a flock of his peers, all talking at once. Complete chaos erupted.

"Manny, howas yer day?"

"Where didja go?"

"You were gone all day, didja meet a big beautiful "she-gull?"

As the choir of voices grew around him, the flock began to echo what became a sort of chant....

"It must have been a girl, what did you do?" "Didja beak her?"

"Beak her" means kiss her in Gull lingo. "Didja beak her?" "Didja beak her?" "Didja beak her?" "Didja beak her?" "Didja beak her?" "Didja beak her?" "Didja beak her? "Didja beak her?" "Didja beak her?" "Didja beak her?" "Didja beak her?"" And so the chant went on, and on, and on.

Manny had enough. He jumped up on an old pylon and flapped his wings furiously, "Silence, please! You guys sit around all day and look for beach scraps. You have no life. I fly out to sea and along the shore lines every day. I exercise and stay in shape. I am well aware human food scraps are not good for me, and I'm very picky about what I eat. When I come home at night, I am usually surrounded by a bunch of gulls that wasted their day, and want the scoop on mine. At first it was fun, but I've learned this is no more than an ego trip. Look, I don't mind sharing. What I'm concerned about is that none of you do anything all day long, and then when I come home you apparently are living vicariously through my adventures. If this were yesterday, I'd say to you come on along and create your own experiences and memories. Out there is a big and beautiful world. Sure it's full of danger, but if I go around worrying about my skin, er...feathers all the time, chances are I wouldn't do anything at all. To me this is worse than the risks I take. At least I have a life guys. You sit all day and watch TV in the confines of your safe nests, and never venture out. Is this what you want for yourselves? The scraps that humans leave behind?

Take a dive man! Find a big fish and bring it home. Adventure out a little. Take a flight. Fly high, you can do it. I do it every day, and today I had the most wonderful adventure of my life. If I hadn't taken a chance and flown a little beyond my limits, I never would have met the most beautiful maiden I have ever seen or known. I was brave and dared to land on the rocks near her and struck up a conversation. We spent all day. My heart was so light by the end of our time together I glided home on calm sea winds and never felt any strain. There you have it. That was my adventure today and why I am so late making it back tonight. Can you guys relate at all? Can you ever think of having lives of your own? I love you all like brothers, but please try to understand, there is an adventure out there for each of you too. Go for it, and maybe real happiness will come your way too."

Manny's throng milled around and rumbled a little. Then one shouted out, "But did you beak her?" And before long the chant was in full bloom once again. Manny did about the same thing Minnie did when he detected his friends didn't understand. He smiled, shook his head and muttered in a subdued voice; "You guys will never learn." Manny launched into the air and flew off toward his humble home to dream about the stars, moon, and mermaid who had awakened a place in his heart he had never known. That night Manny slept well.

4

The next day Manny awakened to an unusually illuminant dank day. The morning sea mist was cool and penetrating. A good day for another adventure Manny thought. Manny decided to stretch out a little and take a short walk on the beach to loosen up. A few other early risers were out walking slowly and absorbing the healing rays of early morning light. Manny noticed a few humans were out early too. It was time to find something nourishing for breakfast. Fresh shells washed up on the beach provided healthy seafood dining. Manny ate a little more than usual because he had a long trip ahead of him again today, and hoped the lofty air currents were strong enough to carry him to his new friend with due speed.

And so the saga of a new day opened its arms to welcome the day's first arrival. Manny rose far above the ocean, and flew higher and higher until he picked up wind currents going out to sea and floated with wings extended to altitudes no other seagull had ever seen. As the air carried him outward, he became more and more relaxed. Over an hour passed when he spotted the place where his dream began. He circled his destination. Minnie had not arrived. Manny landed on their oasis as an agile bird approaching a narrow limb, and waited on the cool rocks in silence for his lady to rise from the depths. While Manny was waiting, he began to feel a little sad. He wondered if Minnie would really show up. After all, she was so beautiful and could have any man she wanted. Why not!? Why should she care for a silly seagull that lives in a boot? The more he thought about it, the sadder he became. At one point he felt foolish and embarrassed for being there. As the sun drenched morning passed, Manny felt a bit colder and anxious. Every moment seemed to be an eternity. He had no idea if or when Minnie would surface. After all, they never set a time. Neither of them owned a watch or could tell time. Time was ascertained in terms of the position of the sun during daylight. Both Manny and Minnie told time by morning noon or night, not by Big Ben. Manny thought he should have at least told Minnie he'd arrive at their meeting place in the morning, but he assumed she was as enthusiastic as him and would be there early. "WHERE ARE YOU

MINNIE?" Manny lamented aloud. "I'll wait here 'til sundown if I need to. I must know for sure."

More time passed. The excitement of anticipation gave way to the boredom of waiting, watching, and occasionally thinking the sounds of the whooshing sea upon the rocks was Minnie about to break the surface. Finally, disappointment and resignation that Minnie is not coming intensified his depression. As despair overcame Manny's heart and pain of unrequited love churned his stomach, his eyes turned red and filled with saltwater tears. Manny fell to his knees and wept into the ocean. From those tears a rainbow was born. It rose up into the sky and gradually illuminated the tender face of Minnie who had risen from the sea and embraced Manny in her arms.

As she embraced him, and wiped away his tears Minnie softly whispered into his ear.

"Manny, did you know, from every tear a rainbow is born?" She smiled, tilted her head and kissed Manny on his soft feathered head. Manny clung to her. He had never loved anyone so much before.

5

After their joyous reunion, Manny and Minnie continued to share for hours as the day passed. Minnie explained why she couldn't make her way to the surface too early for several reasons. Minnie loved to sleep. That was easy. But an early rising could make her certain prey for sharks who feed in the late evening around dusk, and in the morning near sunrise. She cautioned Manny not to dive at these times, or the lunch he sought might eat him! Manny did know about sharks and had seen plenty of them, including a couple close calls.

Today was another day for them to get to know each other and relate their adventures. Manny had so many he didn't know where to start. Diplomatic Minnie resolved his concern; "Then tell me about the most exciting one."

"My most exciting adventure took me all the way across America. The day it began was like any other day. Winds out over the ocean were very strong, like a wave that washes you up on the beach. When I jumped into the air, I was swept into a whirl wind and spun around until I was completely disoriented. I knew I was being carried a great distance, and was completely out of control. I was at the mercy of nature's fury, torn violently from flight and dumped on the deck of a U. S. Navy Battleship far out to sea. I had no idea where I was. The feeling was similar to being caught and flipped by a rip-tide. I staggered to stand, reeling and dizzy. When I got myself under control, I decided to try to make the most of where I was and look around. It wasn't long when I spotted the mess hall. Wow! So much waste, I had a feast. I ate so much I got sea sick. After a short nap atop a railing, I explored the destroyer. It was the first time I ever saw an airplane up close. This is how people fly? They make these machines with big steel wings and loud engines that lift them high into the sky. Of course, I wanted to get a closer look. I wanted to see a fellow bird, one that allegedly swallowed many birds for its fuel. Its stealth presence appeared to be a formidable predator at the very least. I flew over to one of the giant birds and landed near where the pilot steps into the cockpit. I thought I was the only one there when I heard a loud burst from the engines and a thrust that threw me into the back seat of the cockpit. It was un-occupied except for me. Then the glass quickly closed over me and apparently I was trapped inside. I noticed a pilot putting on a helmet and talking into a microphone. The wings that were folded up to the sides began to straighten out and locked into place. Suddenly, the big airship backed up and taxied to a location on the deck where it was held in place while the engines revved to a pitch that hurt my ears. I realized then, I was about to take a ride. This is cool, I thought. I wonder if any other seagull has ever enjoyed this experience without being fried in the engines that is. The straps released at the height of the revving and the airplane shot like a rock from a slingshot, up, up and away!

In only a few seconds we reached the highest I had ever flown. I was rising so fast my stomach almost came up in my throat. Up above the clouds the great bird climbed. This was the ride of my life. The feeling was so exhilarating it took my breath away. Above the clouds the airplane leveled out and almost seemed to stand still. Clouds all around formed giant puffy cotton balls that resembled a variety of shapes. I thought I saw the whole world pass before my eyes in the form of mystical curls. Unbelievable! The sun shone above every cloud brightly, and where the clouds were the thickest, Mr. Sun reflected but didn't penetrate a single ray below. I remember my mother telling me to never forget, when things get tough, I should keep on going, weather the storm and walk through the clouds, because the sun always shines above the clouds, and to find peace and happiness I must first pass thru storm clouds and darkness to arrive on the other side. My quest to find tranquility and warmth in a celestial world revealed its treasured reward and welcomed me into its refuge in the sky. I had to smile as I remembered my wise mom when I realized I was seeing first hand what she described when I was a chicklet.

The next leg of my journey took me to a Grand Harbor where some kind of celebration was being held. When I looked out the window, I saw other airplanes surrounding us in a "V" formation like birds! It was so cool! We streaked over the large city, and up the harbor. The harbor was full of party boats, and people were enjoying good weather and celebrating in a spirit of patriotic pride. It was July 4th in America. Some partiers were jumping in the water and playing games. I bet there was a lot of good food down there for seagulls. I knew where I was because of the big statue my father told me about. He said in a place called New York there's a really large statue of a lady holding a torch and a book. If you ever make it there, be sure to sit right on top of the crown on her head. This is the most beautiful view you will ever have from anything man made. BUT, just remember, do not poop on this statue, someone might shoot at you. It's hallowed ground to humans and you must maintain due reverence and respect.

The jet slowed a bit, and the pilot cracked open the back hatch about a foot. He had spotted me and was trying to get me out of the backseat cockpit. I kept dodging his prodding and lost my balance. The wind sucked me out, and I was spinning out of control. Thank God he had slowed a little, because I was not sucked into his jet engine. Finally, after tumbling again out of control, I regained my air wings and was okay. It came to me, now is the perfect opportunity to do what my father spoke about! I flew back to the giant statue and landed on the very top of her crown. Another of my life's dreams was fulfilled (and I remembered not to poop)! By now, Minnie was looking at Manny with a skeptical amusing smile. Nevertheless, the story was interesting if not a bit humorous.

After enjoying the spectacular view for a very long time, I decided to fly into town and meet some of the local birds. They're called pigeons. Most of them wouldn't give me the time of day. I did meet a young pigeon like myself who couldn't believe I sat on top of the Statue of Liberty and never made a mess. He explained that any pigeon worth his salt would leave behind some sort of mark. After all, that's what pigeons are best known for. The young pigeon's name was Barf. What an odd name. Barf filled me in on the city and all about New Yorkers. We flew together down to a place called Central Park. This was a BIG hang out for pigeons.

It was easy to see why. It seemed to me it was about the only place in the big city that had a lot of trees. Many humans came here in the summer to feed pigeons peanuts and stale bread. An occasional picnic usually left plenty of goodies behind too. Food was plentiful, and there were a lot of pigeons around competing for it. I wasn't sure I'd like the lifestyle, but then I'm a seagull. I liked the freedom of open air, not the enclosed feeling I experienced in the midst of hundreds of high-rises. I hung out with Barf all evening only because I wasn't sure where I was, or was going. I stayed the night in his roost atop a tall building in the middle of town around Broadway and 42nd Street. Barf took me all over the city. I swooped through Times Square, and down past the Garment District, toward South Street Seaport. Then we went over into Greenwich Village, to SoHo and on toward the Jazz clubs in the south end. From there we soared thru China Town to one of Barf's favorite hangouts and dined on some wonderful gourmet Chinese food that had been recently thrown out. We had a great time, but I was so delirious and full of food, I needed a nap. At that point we returned to Barf's roost. Now mind you, I thought city birds should live much better than those of us from the seashore. How wrong! Conditions were crowded and I felt itchy and dirty atop a concrete slab covered with dust and soot. Barf didn't have the greatest TV reception either. The tall buildings around us blocked a lot of signal. I suggested to Barf that he might consider cable. His roost was so small I couldn't imagine how he enjoyed living in such a crowded space. Apparently, Barf was happy. I supposed he never knew any other way of life. Isn't it amazing how we all sort of adapt to where we are and who we are? I understood another lesson I was taught long ago. We are all born with a memory. That is to say, everything we know about life and learn is related to our immediate environment. From the time we are born we are given ideals from our parents, beliefs, and political views by our teachers and those mentor us from within our own immediate sphere of existence. We have our ethnocentric views, strictly environmentally influenced! We expect from life what life has given us, and never in fact know ourselves because we are "made up" of everything else all around us. Know thyself is almost never recognized in the modern world we live in. Where I was that night was living proof. No pigeon was honestly happy. Most had an inherited attitude about living. On the Island I came from, I could have fallen in the same trap. It's so easy to fall back on what we know, and narrow our vision only to our limited perspective. Somehow, I escaped all that. I'm on a journey to the far reaches of the earth. A vagabond in a world divided between order and chaos. Somewhere I picked up the notion that if I ever wanted to find myself as a sentient bird, I need to reach out and experience the world first hand. I need to rise above the flock and proclaim that I, Manny the Seagull, am here for a reason. I have extracted the inundations and conflagrations of environmental memory given to me from birth. I am alone a living creature. I have a right to be here, and will live and cherish every moment I am given to its fullest.

As the sun set over the horizon, I realized how grateful I am every day to be alive. This first part of my once in a lifetime trip gave me a lot to think about. When I am flying high, I'm in awe of the magnificence of the earth in which I was given a place to dwell and be free. Every day is a day of gratitude.

The night was windy, but we survived the swaying high-rise. Early in the morning I bid farewell to Barf and his friends and neighbors. I flew as high as I could, escaped the city, and set off on another day of adventure. The difficult decision for me was to take an inland route. I was accustomed to seeing water all around me and hearing the rhythmic sounds of the ocean and crashing waves. I knew this was a part of what I was born with, and I wanted to experience more. What is it like to be a "land lubber?" Where do they fish? So many questions. Somewhere out there are answers.

6

Manny noticed Minnie appeared distracted. "Minnie. Do you want me to continue?

"Of course I do. I want to hear all about your adventures. It gives me a good feeling that you feel like sharing your experiences with me."

"I'm nothing special Minnie, just another bird on the wall, if you know what I mean. Okay, I'll keep going. I don't want to bore you."

Minnie, nodded her approval, and mused quietly as she admired Manny's regal stature. "Manny is so full of spirit and teeming with a zest for life. I can see it in his eyes."

Manny continued. "Okay, where was I? Oh, yeah. I decided to go inland. I wanted to see how humans live because they're the ones who have dominion over the earth according to what I was taught. The humans I saw in New York had varying degrees of dominion over nothing I witnessed or understood. It was apparent to me they weren't always happy because they try to control everything in their lives including the un-manageable. I didn't see a whole lot of difference between them and pigeons. Maybe as I progress inland I can zigzag through the country, north to south, east to west, and get a better idea of what humans are genuinely like. I certainly don't fancy forming an opinion about the entire species based solely on people from New York.

I departed New York and passed over the State of New Jersey into eastern Pennsylvania. Lots of seagulls flew with me and I didn't feel too out of place or unique.

At this point I made a decision to take in the sights of another great city I had studied in Higull School. Philadelphia. People here are bound to be different than in New York, even though the cities are fairly close in proximity. Philadelphia seemed to be a much brighter city with lots of tourist spots, and where things like the Liberty Bell are on display. I saw them all as only a bird can. I remembered what my dad told me about the big statue, and in accordance with that instruction, I left no unsightly deposits on any monuments. For all the landmarks and marvels I witnessed up to now, I realized I had barely scratched the surface. The magnitude of this venture felt as though a lifetime could be spent getting to California. About the time I was considering my next move a large shaggy seagull named Crusty bellowed into my life. Crusty had a rough voice and his feathers were in a state of permanent disarray. He looked like he had been electrocuted. I believed he passed his prime many years ago. Nevertheless, old Crusty came up with a solution to my little dilemma. I told him what I was up to and he flapped his wings furiously with excitement. "You got a big dream son. How do you think you're gonna carry it out?"

"I have no idea Crusty, any suggestions?"

Crusty uttered two words. "Follow me." We landed on a perch overlooking a massive train yard. "Here's your ticket little buddy. Forget the zigzag stuff and jump aboard one of these going west.

They don't move too fast around cities, and you'll have plenty of time to explore different bergs and towns they pass through. You can always catch another one when you're ready to move on and save some mileage on your wings. You can make it to the west coast in about a week if you so choose, or take your time and explore. You'll see many magnificent sites, and witness a cross section of this great land you'll never forget."

"It sounds as if you've done this before Crusty, is that true?"

"It certainly is, and I highly recommend it. By the way, you might find some good food, especially if you take the passenger trains." That was all I needed to hear. I thanked Crusty for his timely counsel and winged my way toward a large passenger train about to depart.

The trip across the country was filled with adventure. I learned a lot about how people lived surrounded by land rather than water. I breathed in the wide open spaces, hills, trees, forests, and animals I had never seen. Farm lands and miles of crops dotted the country landscape. People travel by cars, trains and airplanes instead of boats. Highways and freeways form a vast linear geometric artwork in a never ending progression crisscrossing the face of the natural topography. By the time the train passed near a city called Pittsburgh, I saw a distinct difference in the way people lived. What's most interesting is that people build homes, live in apartments and condos and many different types of communities. They build their homes to shelter themselves from weather and natural elements. I think man must be the only creature who adapts his environment to his needs and comfort while the rest of us adapt ourselves to the environment we live in. Maybe this is what is meant about the world being man's dominion. If that's the case, I'm confused.

I also met many exotic birds I'd only seen pictures of in books or on the History Channel. I was awed by the salient color and grace of the brilliant red birds called Cardinals. These were splendid creatures, as colorful as many of the tropical varieties I knew. The Cardinals are revered in parts of the Midwest. In Ohio they are the State bird. In St. Louis, Missouri a baseball team is named after them, and in Arizona a football team honors them. I

saw bluebirds too. They're called Blue
Jays. I wondered if they're Canadian
birds, because there's a baseball team
named for them in Toronto. Blue Jays
appear to have a strange disposition. I
suppose because they're Canadian
predators. I can go on and on about
the varieties of finches and large birds
like Turkey Vultures and Eagles I
encountered throughout America, but
the one bird I loved the most was the
soft-spoken placid ringed-neck dove. I
think they may somehow be distantly
related to seagulls. I met my first dove
near a small town in southern Indiana
going due west. The Dove's name was
Buddha. Why in the world would any
self respecting bird want to name their
son Buddha? It made no sense.
Buddha was sitting in a maple tree near
the roof of an old abandoned barn

located along side a narrow two lane secondary road. The barn was painted on one side all black with big yellow letters that said "Chew Mail Pouch." I didn't understand that either. Why would anyone want to chew a mail pouch? I guessed I had a lot to learn and decided to strike up a conversation with him. I was much larger than Buddha, and when I flew in and landed on the branch next to where he was roosting (quietly meditating) he almost had a heart attack. We exchanged names, species, and greetings after he settled and caught his breath.

For several hours we swapped stories about our lives. I was amazed at how much Buddha was like me, excepting he knew a lot more. Buddha was a genuine treasure trove of wisdom and life experience, and a one bird course in

American History. He seemed to know everything about everywhere I was headed. Buddha was extremely accommodating. He offered me a place to stay for the night with him and his family. Buddha was a family bird, and although he enjoyed being a guy and "doing guy things," he faithfully returned home to the love of his life each and every day. "Let's go out to dinner," he proclaimed. "We'll go in style, and you can experience first hand how we country folk get along." What a great idea. I had never been to a bird café, and I looked forward to the country dining encounter. Buddha and I flew over to his nest and he introduced me to his lovely wife Charlotte and children, uhh chicklets. He had three little hairless babies, only about a week old. Their names were Cindy, Gwen, and Becket. Two girls and a boy. Their home wasn't high up in the tree, and was very secluded. According to Buddha, it was a safer haven for his family and less obvious to the ever prowling Canadian Blue Jays. Before we left for the Café, the neighbor lady named Thea came over to sit with the little ones. She was referred to by Buddha and Charlotte as "Ms. Red Feet," because she was always saying she didn't trust anyone with red feet, namely pigeons and their relatives. I thought that was sort of strange. Aren't doves related to pigeons?

The name of the restaurant we were going to dine in was "Feathers Cafe." A menu was posted in the window. I stood on a perch and read the choices. I couldn't believe a little country restaurant like this had such a great menu. It was filled with seafood and good seed choices including pre-digested and freshly regurgitated delicacies! I was getting hungry. The café was abuzz with guests. Perches were set up in rows with dining troughs fastened to the front for individual dining. About fifty varieties of birds flying around with a purpose made lots of noise and added to the ambiance. The club was filled with music provided by a live entertainment Jazz and Light Rock group. How cool is this?! The name of the musical group was the "The Buzz." They opened their first set with their theme song Lullaby of Birdland. On drums was a wild Vulture named Roadkill. The bass guitar was a big Grackle named Goobird, on piano a genius Robin named Wormer, lead guitar was a big goose named Neck (or Nick), and of course the star vocalist, a tiny Humming Bird named Honey. She flitted all over the club and serenaded anyone who smiled and tipped her with something special like seeds, bugs or worms for the band members, a dead rat for the drummer, or a flower for her to insert her beak into and snort the aromatic pollen. Roadkill performed a special song called the Buzzard Ballad. It was hilarious, and the words reminded me a little of myself. The first verse went like this:

*"Buzzard, Buzzard in the sky,
put some whitewash in my eye.
I won't sigh and will not cry,
I'm just glad that cows don't fly."*

The Host who seated us was a dark mysterious Raven who looked at us as if we were about to become the main course rather than eat the main course. He was a little scary but very professional and dignified. After being seated a penguin waiter entered the scene. What the heck was a penguin doing in this part of the country? If I analyze this properly penguins come from the Antarctic. This means they migrate to the United States and come from south to north, not north to south. They probably ride a few icebergs into the ocean and make their way to the southern tip of South America. From there a Penguin migrates north through South America into Central America, and then through Mexico. He must then cross a border between Mexico and the United States in order to get into the country. I suppose they are required to obtain a green card, because they can't fly over the border and must walk across like everyone else. Mmm...I presume if they get here without a green card we could call them "Illegal Avians?" It seems like a lot of hassle to migrate such a great distance to find work. Evidently, the tips are good from mainland birdland restaurants, because a lot of penguins have migrated from the Antarctic for better wages and better weather. It only makes sense. We had a great time. It was a first for me. Good food, good wine, and good fellowship. It doesn't get any better than that. Buddha loved his Italian food, and had a big dish of "bird spaghetti," that is steamed earthworms in tomato sauce, garnished with a large road apple meatball. Charlotte was more conservative; she dined on greens and seeds. I splurged on the local seafood, sunfish in lemon sauce, garnished with creek-bed snails. We drank fresh concord wine picked from the local grapevines to wash it down. When finished, we ordered their special desert. It was listed on the menu as Crème Burleigh of Assorted Bugs, with little trails of chocolate forming a happy face over the encrusted ants imbedded in the upper crystallized layer. The experience was enchanting.

When we left the Café a long walk was in order. As the sun began to set, it was time to return home with Buddha and Charlotte. I slept soundly that night, felt safe, and was happy I met these peaceful creatures. An uncomplicated evening with these laidback mid-west doves was the highlight of my trip so far.

7

The next day came too soon. Cool nights and warm days in the Midwest are something else. It's so much easier to sleep and awaken refreshed when the temperature is a little cool. I woke up to the smell of fresh fried earthworms. No, birds don't eat bacon and especially don't eat eggs (excepting those mean blue jays)! I can't imagine anyone eating eggs. Too much like cannibalism!   Fresh hot spring water tea was served with the earthworms. What a delectable combination. I realized, because of my size, I ate more than Buddha's entire family. Buddha begged me to stay on another day and I told him I needed to move on before I ate them out of house and home. I bid farewell to my feathered friends and prepared to depart. Buddha flew a little distance with me toward the train yard. Before I departed he decided to wait with me for the arrival of the next train.

"Manny, before I met Charlotte and settled down I wanted to travel the globe and see the many spectacles our world had to offer. I couldn't do that because my life changed abruptly one day. My father was hunted down by blue jays and extinguished. His last fighting breath was spent protecting my mom and me. Mom was attacked too, but after they took daddy down we managed to escape. Mom was injured and I spent the rest of her life caring for her, hunting food for her, and tending to her needs. On that fateful day she not only lost the love of her life she suffered losing her vision in the violent attack. In the years that followed I took care of mom and learned numerous lessons from her. I was amazed at how she described every detail of her relationship with dad and remembered everything she had ever done and seen with such precise clarity. One thing she told me I will never forget. I want to share this with you as you prepare to move on. When mom had something important to say, she leaned in the direction she was speaking and cocked her head with a loving smile. By the way, dad thought I had that smile too when I was born. This is why I was named Buddha. Anyway, she said she learned to appreciate and savor every moment in her life. "If I had full sight,

and knew tonight I was going blind, I'd
take a lasting and completely consuming
view of my visual world. I would see as
I've never seen before, every cloud
formation in the heavens, every rain
drop and every flower in the meadow. I
would want to make sure I knew the
sweet fragrance of every pine, and
beheld the splendor of the stately and
unyielding oak. Having advanced
knowledge of my impending blindness,
I'd perceive every treasure on earth
through my inner eyes. As I
approached eternal darkness, my
memories would then be fulfilled when I
understood all this is in me no matter
where I go or what I cannot see. Now,
when I look to my inner-reflection I find
peace in the valley of my heart. Never
am I frustrated by not being able to see,

because I am too busy being grateful for all that I have seen."

"Manny, as you prepare to fly into the horizon, don't look, but see. See with your heart, feel with the passion for life you are given. If your life ends tomorrow your heart will be at peace. You'll follow the course of great rivers, and fly over a wide awesome canyon. You will witness sunlight reflecting from the face of massive fields of golden wheat and all life will teem with clarity and dimension here before incomprehensible. At your journey's end you will achieve enlightenment and understand what you have been given. Your life will know a new purpose when you discover you are a part of this grand plan. Never look back if you must stare. Move onward and upward. Your vision will be much greater than your eyes, and you will find true wisdom in your heart beyond the most eloquent words ever framed. To quote Aristotle, "Know thyself." Know thyself first and create your own vision of the world within you. Trust and understand this wisdom with your heart. Transcend the feathers that adorn you. Be a spirit on a bird's quest first, and a bird second. With this trust, you will find your spirituality however you define it, and it will be your reality. All else is fantasy. Now go in peace Manny, and never have the kind of day others may ordain. Have the kind of life YOU want."

Without another word Buddha lifted his wings and flew away. I felt I finally understood why his given name was Buddha. My train arrived. I winged my way to one of the cars. Everything in the earth around me seemed to have a

peculiar dreamlike glow. That day I
became one with my world.

8

I knew I was heading west and had no
idea where I was going to wind up. I
liked that. I wanted the surprise of
seeing the world through eyes of inquiry
and astonishment. The train lumbered
down the tracks and off into a new day.
As miles streaked by, the landscape
appeared so vast and extensive it
turned into a blur. I spotted a large
freeway, I–70 west. Before long, the
train passed directly through a little
farming town called Abilene, Kansas. As
best as I could make out, it appeared to
have a church or an antique shop on
every corner as I passed through. I
stopped here to explore a little, and
found an old saloon where Wild Bill

Hickok was shot and the remnants of an ancient Wild West town. It was a fun place to explore. I observed how arid weather dries out and ages wood when I landed on a hitching post and it collapsed under my light weight. Nothing withstands time and nature. Only legends and ruins give way to the colorful past of the Wild West. That built by man eventually dissolves into the earth, and makes me wonder why they are taught to build for the future. All things erected for immortality fall prey to the scythe of time. Is anything built with human hands everlasting? My transport train continued and didn't stop again until it was near a town called Colorado Springs. I jumped off and decided to take a closer look. This town was home of the Air Force Academy and Pike's Peak. As I was flying over the east end, I saw what appeared to be a tourist area called Garden of the Gods. Garden of the Gods is a collection of jutting rocks and cliffs seeming to protrude directly upward from the earth. The jutting rocks had the appearance of giant monoliths, thus the origin of the name. As I recall, these huge slabs were a reddish color when in direct sunlight. Most of the rocks were navigable by tourists. Panoramic painted vistas popped up around every bend. In a remote garden of protruding rocks I met my first Eagle. What an imposing creature! His name was Sam, as in Uncle Sam. Sam was a Bald Eagle and a Native American Bird. I wished I had talons like Sam's, especially when diving for a large fish dinner. Utoh! (Manny looked at Minnie and decided he better amend his sentence) I mean when carrying things back to my little nest, you know, like new electronic stuff, I-Pod, cell phone, and so on (nervously). What a beak for cracking seashells. I want a schnozzle like that too! Size and wing span of the Great Eagle were impressive. I bet no one messes with a bird like Sam, although he appeared to be a gentle sort. Sam was a Senior Avian, and because of his stature, carried his weight and size rather well. Sam was eager to show me around. I felt safe flying next to him. He took me up and down the slopes and cliffs of Pike's Peak, and spread his giant wings for the throngs of tourists with cameras. I tried my best to talk to him when we rested, but Sam was a bird of few words. He made the same offer for me to stay with his family for the night and dine with them as Buddha did two days before. I felt honored and couldn't say no. I realized he'd probably serve a small mammal for dinner, like a rat or possum, or something he picked-up from the desert floor comparable to a big jack rabbit or prairie dog. I wasn't too thrilled, however, I felt should gracefully accept his offer if I wanted to make the next leg of my trip. Deep in the back of my mind, I wondered if Sam was contemplating seagull stew for dinner. I trusted him and took a leap of faith! Sam was married to an amazing lady named Betsy, and father of two large and hungry chicks named George and Abe. Their nest was large. I could lose my entire entertainment center and water bed in one corner. It rested on a jutting rock ledge high up on the side of a cliff overlooking the Colorado River. A magnificent view! I called this dwelling the Eagle's Penthouse. We didn't dine out either, which was alright with me. I merely wanted to enjoy the warm breeze, towering view, and relax. As dusk gave way to night the stars became incredibly clear, and I felt that if I reached up and touched the heavens I could pluck out a beautiful shiny ornament. Sam made his way to where I was sitting. "What you lookin' at Manny?"

"Sam, only a couple of days ago I was flying high in this same sky. Isn't it interesting that during the day, our one sun lights up everything? At night there are literally millions of points of light, and yet the sky remains black except where the moon and the stars shine. I suppose the sun is so large and radiates so much light, you can't see anything else. At night, you take away the sun and see everything! What do you think of that Sam?"

"Not sure what you're driving at Manny.

"Well, when you take away the sun, where do all those stars come from? I think that's what I'm trying to figure out."

"I think I may know the answer to your question Manny. It's in the form of an old Native American legend. It is called the "Legend of the Trees."

"Huh, what do trees have to do with stars?"

"Be patient Manny and I'll tell you about the legend. It will open your eyes and you'll see stars as you have never seen them before. Many moons ago it began when the first people of the earth gained dominion over all things. In those days it was believed the Great

Spirit lived in the trees because trees whisper at night, and give shelter and warmth by day when the seasons are cold. Our fathers discovered that fallen trees, dry and rotting, made the best fuel for the nighttime sun. The "fire" of warmth and light was discovered by the first ancient Medicine Man of our Lodge. Fires from torches lit the way at night and opened their eyes to darkness. A divine spirit lived within every tree, and was given to us by the Great Spirit as the Spirit of Light. Like the trees, we knew the Spirit of Light resided within us too, and gave us numerous visions and wisdom to the ancient wise warriors over many moons. The Great Spirit needed a way to give every lodge in every tribe the same wisdom of light to share equally. A hope for harmony between tribes was the desired result.

For the Great Spirit this was easy, but he needed our help. It was long believed that all our fathers were particles of the great creation, each containing a glimmer of the Great Spirit's eternal flame. This is our definition of the essence of life. It's what gives us dominion over the Animal People. To expand our gift of fire, the Great Spirit decided to capture the blaze within each living being and share it with all. At death, it was presumed the fire within us is snuffed out. It is not. It waits for the Great Spirit to re-consume every particle. The Great Spirit chose his warrior and instructed him to spread his wisdom to every lodge in every tribe. These are His words. "When our eyes have clouded over, and from our hands have dropped the working tools of life, know that I have directed the living light within them to enter into the trees. Therefore, take the hand of the fallen, whether in war or peace, and build a pyre. Deposit their remains there, and the light of their Spirits will enter every living tree as a million fireworks depart the pyres. Now when the life of a tree ends, it has become heavy with spirits and falls to the ground. Logs from these fallen trees are given to warm you and to open your vision into the night. You will notice many sparks leave your campfires and rise into the heavens. When they are very high they appear to burn out and disappear. They have not disappeared, but rise miles further into the heavens, and in an instant relight the sky as stars. These are spirits released from the trees. What we thought to be our offering was in truth a gift to us. They dwell in the trees we send up and return illumination to our eyes. These stars are our forefathers watching us, guiding us and lighting darkness from above. Whenever you look up at night you will know stars in a different way. Our fathers and their fathers before them are our guardians and beacons. The Legend of The Trees is our hope, and with this hope we find harmony in all things."

9

I slept under the eyes of the stars that night. From the ledge morning came with an invigorating chill. The sun rose quickly and warmed me throughout. As I stretched and spread my wings, I began to understand why I was making this trek. The Great Spirit Sam referred to was educating me. I learned new lessons, met different species of my own kind, and absorbed insight from every encounter. I knew somehow, someday I might find a great truth and share it with my offspring, or anyone who chose to listen. I suspected there to be a more important reason for these experiences. For now, it was a matter of getting through the day and letting the energy and vibrations of the unknown guide me. Adaptation to the ebb and flow of life, time and change seemed to be goal enough. Sam wanted me to stay another day. I knew I needed to take to the sky and let the synchronization of the real universe echo within my nature and steer me. This is how I kept going, for then the world was beneath my humble talons. I bid farewell to another new friend, and flew into the endless beyond to the local train yard. "All aboard," the Conductor called. I boarded and departed Colorado Springs.

The further west I traveled, the more I took side trips. I wanted to see Mount Rushmore, a monument to great Americans. It was so far away I decided not to go in that direction. I was afraid I'd be tempted to leave my mark on the old weathered rock and deface a great monument. It was too inviting. Instead, I flew further southwest until I reached Arizona and the Grand Canyon. Here I eye-witnessed the most spectacular structure on earth carved from native rock by nature. I'm lucky I'm only a bird, because I wasn't limited to breathtaking views from ledges and barriers. I flew out over the great

canyon and followed the river below. I
spent the next several days exploring on
my own and never felt alone or lonely
for conversation. I was beginning to
learn to respect who I am and what I
could do. I liked my own presence and
understood the reasoning was
something I heard before. As I am in
silent flight, I've learned to quietly pass
into my most acute awareness.
Through this awakening, another world
is opened and every new dawn brings
new enlightenment. I'm grateful, in
view of the fact this is how I ultimately
discover who I really am. I missed the
cities a little and some of the hustle and
bustle of "doing life." In the Grand
Canyon I didn't feel I was defacing
anything when I deposited my
whitewash on the canyon walls. I was
adding ambiance, (smile)!

The rocky formations carved by wind, rain and natural erosion were no less impressive than the formations of clouds in the sky. My imagination saw great Native American Warriors frozen in rock. The history and mystery of the world was preserved in moments of time piled layer upon layer for us to uncover. Natural events forming the elements and sculptures we know today were clearly evident. Experiencing the Grand Canyon from the vantage point of my wings was more than dreamlike. In those moments I felt a certain awe I can't express in words. I remembered something my father told me the day I took my first flight from the nest. He said, "Your life will not be measured by the number of breaths you take my son. It will be measured by the moments that take your breath away. Now fly son. Fly high and away." Today, I understand what he meant.

I continued on and winged my way upward until I caught a crosswind that carried me into a narrow canyon. I literally gasped at the site ahead. It was the most massive manmade monolith I had ever seen, Hoover Dam. I flew over the dam and up the canyon. If that thing ever cut loose, there'd be an ocean in the desert! It was so perfect, nestled in the rocks, and spanning all the way across the canyon. This structure ought to be one of the seven manmade wonders of the world. I can barely imagine what it took to build it.

I flew directly over the top where tourists were gathered on both sides between fences looking over and taking pictures. As I drew in closer, I noticed there weren't any concrete signatures I could readily see. I remember when I was a little bird I flew into town once and saw a couple of men repairing a sidewalk. They poured new concrete in the "jack hammered" faults, and smoothed them over. When finished, the sidewalk appeared as good as new. I remember one of the workers taking his fingers and putting down his name and year of the repair. He remarked to the other worker, "All concrete should have a name etched in it somewhere, it's a tradition," he laughed.

My wheels were turning. This massive structure contained no signatures. What a shame. The concrete is dry now and we can't even put bird footprints in it. Mmmmmm (thinking). It isn't a monument, it's a dam. Maybe it would be okay to... Minnie looked at me, smiled, and shook her head no. I guess I'll leave that part out of my story.

I flew further into the Mojave Desert and located my train going west. So far I had traveled nearly straight across the country. I landed in New York, traveled through New Jersey, and all the way across Pennsylvania, through the northern part of West Virginia, through the Buckeye State, Ohio, then Indiana, Southern Illinois, Missouri, Kansas, Colorado, Utah, Arizona, and into Nevada. Next stop is Las Vegas. From there I planned on making my way to San Francisco and the west coast. I was about three-quarters of the way across the continent with a long way to go.

The Western United States was arid and dry compared to the east coast. I decided to get off the train, because I was feeling as though my mouth was full of dust and my eyes were watering from wind and sand kicked up as we sped along the rail. I tried flying and resting at intervals, but was expending too much energy. I finally decided to jump on top of a semi-truck. It was much slower than the train, but easier to travel on and regain my strength. I think the sight of a seagull in the middle of a desert riding a semi was exceptionally odd. As the truck approached the city, I flew off and headed directly west. The rest on the "semi" was refreshing and I felt good as I bounded upward until I located a crosswind that carried me nearly all the way to my next destination.

I could tell I had arrived in Las Vegas because I recognized the hotels like Desert Inn, Caesar's Palace, and a few others I had heard about. It took me more than a day to get there from the time I left the semi. By then, I was hungry, hot, dirty and tired! I took a long and cool bath in a fountain in front of the Imperial Palace.

In the refuge of a shady palm near the fountain I met a young and beautiful Sea Gull named Ida Hoe. Ida was a West Coast Girl. I heard Gulls were extra large on the west coast. She was a large lady, about twice my size. I can see how Alfred Hitchcock was inspired to make a movie about "The Birds." He probably observed sea gulls in many countries, but these large guys took the cake! Though Ida was big she was attractive and made up. I think she wanted to look like a "Show Gull" or something. The end of her beak was caked with bright red lipstick and she must have been wearing about a pound of rouge to enhance her face. She wore false eyelashes over her big dark eyes, and was adorned with so much costume jewelry I wondered how she flew.

"How ya doin' little man? You wanna come up and see me sometime? My name is Ida. Ida Hoe. I'm a material girl, and lookin' for new material, if ya know what I mean.   What's your name handsome?"

"Uh, not sure how to respond, but my name is Manny. I'm flying across America and Las Vegas was one of my destinations. Would you like to show

me around? We could catch some lunch
if you know of any good Bird Bistros?
I'd like to go to a Casino too. I've never
been inside one and...and maybe we
could catch a show live too."
Ida studied me curiously, and finally
responded. "Okay, let's do it...just
follow me and I'll show you a good
time." Away we flew.
Ida decided we should eat first so we'd
have energy for the tour.
Space is limited on the strip. Ida flew
directly to the only club catering strictly
to birds. The Bird of Paradise Hotel,
Restaurant, Lounge, and Casino was a
one stop drop(ping) for wealthy and
well known birds. The most colorful and
flamboyant of the avian genre came
here to gamble, relax and be seen.
Apparently Ida Ho was very popular.
About every male bird acknowledged

her presence. The setting of the restaurant was outside. Gilded perches were provided for the guests. A beautiful fountain of chocolate covered baby tarantulas complemented the setting of the dining area in its midst. It was bordered with exotic tropical plants inhabited by colorful little finches and parrots to add color. Of course, we were greeted and seated on a very comfortable perch overlooking all the activity. Little "bus" birds (sparrows) flitted around everywhere cleaning troughs and setting them for customers as they arrived. The towering Raven was the Mater Dee and presided over the activity to insure every need of every client was attended to. As before, dignified formally attired Penguins were the waiters. We ordered fresh spring water to drink and raw Oysters

Rockefeller for appetizers. Afterward, we dined on a five course gourmet dinner consisting of grub worm salad, escargot with grivet for digestion, an entrée of raw salt-water crab garnished with seaweed, hash brown scallops, and a large fresh chambered nautilus stuffed with lobster meat to round out the side dishes. For desert we enjoyed hot caramel covered raw crawdads sprinkled with coconut. I never ate so much in all my life. Each portion was served separately and kept warm. I was ready for a nap, and my new friend Ida was ready to do the town.

As I struggled to carry my full tummy out of the dining area, I noticed a bird I had never seen. It was extraordinary, and looked like the NBC logo when it fanned its feathers. Ida told me it was a Peacock. She knew them all, and added that peacocks are all show and no go. "You can't trust them, and they will cheat you out of everything you have if you're not careful." Our next stop was the Casino. Can you imagine a bird casino? Lined up in about ten rows were over a hundred "One Clawed Bandits" for us to dump our money (seed) into. In the main body of the casino were dozens of gambling tables with everything from Blackjack to Dice tables and Roulette. I did pretty well at the One Clawed Bandits, but lost it all on Roulette. Ida did much better. She seemed to know when to quit while she was ahead. We spent most of the rest of the evening in the casino and took in a show just after dark. The show was about as colorful as the restaurant. It featured a chorus line of pink flamingos, and a Yellow Canary Pop Singer who whistled the most melodious tunes you ever heard. The main attraction was a Comedian Toucan named Jimmy D. What a Schnauzola that guy had! Jimmy told one joke after another and kept us in stitches. To end the show, a great Buzzard came on stage as a Magician and made a rabbit disappear before our eyes. It was kind of disgusting, but was magical to witness such a devouring disappearing act and grand finale to a supreme evening of entertainment.

At the end of the evening Ida and I departed and flapped our wings, shook feet and bid each other adieu. I thanked Ida for showing me around and spending the day with me. Somehow, I felt this type of life was okay to experience once, but was definitely too rich for my wings. I spent the night near the fountain where I met Ida and departed early the next morning.

10

I felt a little empty when I left Vegas, maybe because my pockets were about empty. I spent more birdseed there than anywhere else on the entire trip. Next destination was California, across the mountains and on to San Francisco. I was eager to see the skyline and fly over the streets of the storied metropolis. I made my way via train and truck almost all the way. From my vantage point, I ascended north and westward over rolling hills and remember how the massive skyline revealed itself like a cinema zoom from a distance to fill the screen with a birds eye panoramic view of the city. The Golden Gate Bridge in the foreground looked more like a footbridge over San Francisco Bay. Today was picturesque. The sunlight reflecting from the bay filled with leisure craft and tankers reminded me of resort areas near the large port cities in the east. It particularly reminded me of the most awe inspiring spectacle I had ever seen when I entered the "Allegheny Tunnel" (by accident) in Pittsburgh, and the unparalleled vista I experienced when it opened at the other end. My vision over San Francisco matched it. The airstream was strong and I had to work to find a place atop the Golden Gate to oversee the city and not be carried off by spiraling twisting gusts.

San Francisco is one very large and beautiful city. Only in the inner city did I see a preponderance of pigeon paint.

The streets are devoid of trash for the most part, and there isn't much to snack on. The piers are all "bustled" with humans enjoying the attractions of the fish market, fine restaurants and shops. I spent the day going from market to market, store to store and seeing every attraction imaginable. I observed lots of seals packed like sardines on the boardwalk piers lounging near the water. They constantly flopped on and off piers looking for morsels and scraps of fish waste dumped into the water by fishermen. That afternoon I took a short flight up Lombard Street, the world's most winding street. I was dizzy by the time I had zigzagged from bottom to top. I flew to the top of Coit Tower and took in another panoramic view of San Francisco Bay from a closer vantage point.

From Coit Tower I spotted Alcatraz, and decided to visit. I can't imagine EVER breaking human laws and being pent up in a place like this. I'm a free bird, not a jail bird. I thrive on the freedom of flight and the wide open spaces. Even humans must fall into a deep despondency when sent to places like this. Humans, in my understanding, are built for freedom too. How can people commit crimes against society which result in confinement and complete physical restriction? I suppose they believe crime pays. Alcatraz stands as testimony that it doesn't. After I paid my respects to Alcatraz and deposited a large quantity of seagull whitewash down one of the walls, I quickly departed. I didn't feel the least bit guilty leaving my graffiti offering!

My next stop was China Town.   Every bird in the world should see China Town in San Francisco. What an inconceivable experience! The city is abundant with medium size buildings to poop on, fabulous restaurants, and especially tolerant people.

Atop one of the buildings I was greeted by a very large West Coast Gull. His name was Dali. He explained he was descendent from a rare species of Tibetan Mountain Gull and crossed with the Great San Francisco Chinatown Gulls. In other words he was an Amerasian Bird. The species is called Yamas. Every Gull of this genus uses two names, their first name followed by species name as last. This may be stretching things a little. Thus, his full name was "Dali Yama." Though it sounded like a strange name for a bird, it sort of had a familiar ring."

In the middle of the sentence Manny sensed he was losing Minnie. Her eyes were drooping, and her fishtail was switching like a restless cat. His story was beginning to sound more like a "fishtail" itself. Manny suddenly felt self-conscious and stuttered a little.

"Well Minnie, I think I've said enough, maybe too much. I'll finish by saying I think I'm a pretty lucky bird. I've traveled the globe and lived through countless diverse encounters. I've shared the best part of it with you, and don't want to ruin it with more long-winded detail. I better quit while I'm ahead."

Manny forced a sheepish restrained smile and sat down quietly.

Minnie blinked a little when she observed Manny as he spoke. His mannerisms and gestures were graceful and manly. She was beginning to feel her own feelings about her new friend. "I'm so awed by your travels and all the friends you've made around the world. I feel special that you want to share them with me."
"I never intended to go so long Minnie. I want to hear about your life too. What does a Mermaid do? Where are you from, and where do you live?"

11

"Gosh Manny, I'm not sure where to begin, but I'll try. Mermaids are born at sea. We are descendents of a mammal called Manatee or Sea Cow. When newly born, we are actually manatees. Because we're mammals, we often attract stray human souls which enter into our bodies. As soon as this occurs a dreamlike transformation takes place and a Mermaid creature is created. We are half Manatee and half Human. Not every manatee gets a human soul. It's a random occurrence and probably some sort of evolutionary throw-back. But it does happen. Eventually, the gray skin and other manatee features such as whiskers and long noses are replaced. We take on human features and become the most beautiful creatures on earth with long flowing hair, well formed bosoms and soft smooth skin. We have both lungs and gills, and a long flowing fishtail. Our legends teach us Mermaids are destined for a special purpose. Unfortunately, so far no one knows what or why. The legend explains Mermaids were created outside normal evolutionary processes. We supposedly are assigned a particular function and will someday change the world when it most needs it. We were created to be living breathing entities with the ability to transcend boundaries of time, space and dimension. Mermaids, it is said, bridge water and land, and will someday, *s o m e d a y* take to the sky. At that point we will be set on a new path to enlighten the world. I have no idea what this all means, but am assured it's true by my mentors."

"I was born under the submerged continent of Atlantis in a place called the Crystal Cave. The Crystal Cave is a complicated structure of underwater caverns winding beneath the continent for hundreds of miles. It's hard to imagine if you've never been there. The caverns rise up hundreds of feet and the walls are imbedded with precious stones, jewels, and shiny crystal. The Crystal Cave, where I was born and now live, is located more than twenty-thousand leagues beneath the abyss. No human or sea gull has ever been there. I would love to show you the neighborhood I was born in, but I'm afraid it's impossible because of extreme water pressure at those depths. Once you are there, however, air pressure is normal. The problem is getting there. Extreme water pressure will crush anyone not acclimated to it. I was a baby when I was chosen to become a Mermaid. I don't remember very much, but was allowed to ascend into the consciousness of the human who was coming into me. I can only imagine what it's like Manny to fly through the heavens and ride the winds. It must be exhilarating. I vaguely remember traveling high above the sea and diving into the ocean to bring my Spirit to life. I was transformed into pure energy. My human essence spiraled into a blinding light and struck the ocean like a laser beam or bolt of lightning piercing the depths. In an instant it was fused with a baby manatee at her very moment of birth. A warm bond was formed which gave the baby manatee breath and awareness. I will never forget that moment. Many moments were vague then, but that was the most vivid moment I ever experienced until, until, uh (spoken very softly) *I met you Manny."*

A moment of awkward silence ensued then Minnie continued. "Over the millennia, since the earth was formed, the Crystal universe came into being long before the fall and sinking of Atlantis. The world was dominated by a human race which wasn't completely developed. Humans in those days were war like creatures that barely stood erect. About the only difference from then to today is that ancient humans were less advanced, however, more civilized than those in our modern world. The ancients lived in land caves and developed a primitive social structure. Fire, wheels and tools were discovered. An early industrial revolution was born. As centuries passed "people" became more sophisticated and developed bigger and better ways of waging war. What followed was a holocaust, and total destruction. Wars, pollution and constant pounding of Terra Fermi's crust finally gave way under its own weight to a horrible doom wrought by evil forces. The planet collapsed upon itself, and the axis's shifted causing great floods and damnation to all living creatures. The earth became void and dark from massive dust storms and volcanic eruptions that blocked the last ray of sunlight. No life survived. Under the calm of the ocean's placid waves

Atlantis sank from the surface and was no more. The only species remaining were the citizens of the sea. Crystal Cave became the last haven for life. Never has war entered these hallowed passageways. We know only peace. By the grace of isolation tranquility rules our world. Today the seas are repopulated and man has been reborn. Unfortunately, not much changed. None of us want to see this happen again. To make a difference and change the world is something Mermaids are supposed to do according to lore. We patiently wait and hope this deep truth will soon be revealed. Time is running out."

Minnie smiled and slowly closed and opened her eyes dreamily envisioning her far away realm.

"I'll attempt to describe the Crystal Cave to you Manny. First, imagine yourself at night skimming the surface of the water while in flight, and flip over like a stunt pilot. Glide with your front side up and gaze at the millions of stars in the sky above. They will pass by quickly and form patterns not unlike streaks of random lights. This is what it's like all the time in our home. The sun doesn't penetrate twenty-thousand leagues down, but the reflections from the surface carry to the outer reaches of the brilliant crystals that line the entrance to the Crystal Universe. These reflections are refracted and sped up, because light is trapped and can only continue to bounce and speed up as they are hurled into the depths like so many speeding bolts of lightning. The illumination pulsates and gets brighter as it travels through. Lightning then turns into shooting stars and brightens our space in a way that gives us warmth, color, beauty and art all rolled into one. The cave itself is divided into many mansions. It's multi-layered, and dives beyond measured depths to the very center or core of the earth. Light dissipates when it exits through molten eruptions. As I said before, the walls are lined with crystal and precious jewels. Many of these have been sculpted into mammoth works of art, some as long and wide as the entire cavern. These are detailed with depictions of history of our universe and our legends. Each facet is incredibly engraved in intricate detail. Many of our artworks have taken centuries to craft. Every iota of our art is dedicated to the peace and exquisiteness in which we live. As young Mermaids, we are permitted to swim anywhere within the confines of our universe at any time without fear of finding harm's way. This is how we are educated. We learn through experience and by subjection to the numerous artifacts and artworks which surround and enhance our every waking moment."

"Plant and animal life is quite different too. Since we have no war or outer conflict, residents (both plant and animal) will tend toward an emphasis on color and aesthetics, not camouflage. We are not influenced by a lack of direct sunlight, because there is no lack of light. It "appears" differently, that's all. Our plant life is complex and extensive beyond imagination. Large communities of multi-colored coral and deep green growth sway in the currents of the chasm. Long tentacles stretch out as if reaching for the sky. There is no confinement to distance and space. Some coral species actually stretch for miles unbroken. The landscape is much more complicated than the world of the human. There is no horizon line and no beginning or end to the panorama of vegetation moving in analogous patterns to the ocean currents. Everything in our Crystal Universe is in harmony, and moves as if dancing with invisible hosts from a time long past although not yet at hand. Likewise, our animal life is exceedingly well developed. There is no need for animals to cultivate or evolve elaborate defense mechanisms. No protective outer skeletal armor is required. Our natural predators are a simple consequence of the food chain. That's all. Animals have progressed along lines of art, attractiveness and color. Can you imagine a translucent dolphin comparable in skin tone to a Jellyfish? Reflections of light on their surface reveals how they are made, where all their organs are located, and reflect a most dynamic array of coloration. When no need to live in fear exists, there is no need to consider anything other than uninhibited natural subsistence. Our evolution is most advanced because of a unique environment within our unassuming caverns. The undersea is pure and clean beyond the reaches of those polluted by humanoids. And Manny, even a seagull can't poop on anything in the Crystal Cave.

As for me, about nineteen years ago I was born. A Mermaid's life span is similar to human life in every respect. I am, therefore, considered young and impressionable. I realize this and strive to learn as much as I can in order to become savvy in the ways of the world. I believe I am a very lucky human, or fish...whatever. When I reached eighteen, I was finally allowed to venture beyond my own world. It doesn't appear there's much for me to do in your world Manny. I really can't walk because of my fishtail. I have no wings and am unable to fly, although I do dream about flying. I can sunbathe. I have different "spots" I go to where humans are unlikely to see me, and this is where I spend my time with other mermaids dreaming and talking about life, love and fantasy. We have a few amazingly good restaurants too. Of course, the ambiance is colorful, bright and well orchestrated. My cuisine is rather different from yours. I mean to say, each creature will have a menu appropriate to their diets, excepting sharks of course. They are not allowed in our dining establishments because they want to eat the patrons! Most restaurants are run by Dolphins. The waiters are only the most agile octopi. Clown fish and colorful angel fish provide entertainment. In the Crystal Cave, each dwelling has cable television and we keep track of weather patterns and (ocean) current events. While we are sunning on the rocks, we solve the world's problems and build a perfect dream world for humankind in the image of the one in which we live. It never seems to work out though. I'm not sure why. In any case, I hope I didn't bore you. We are fairly normal creatures by our standards, and live one day at a time hoping for fulfillment of prophesies and legends in our lifetimes as so many have dreamed before us. There isn't much else to add. I hope you aren't disappointed."

"Your life is enriched with peace and harmony Minnie. You must be a very happy little Mermaid."
"Mostly."
"Mostly? What do you mean Minnie"?
"There is one thing missing in the life of each and every Mermaid."
"What Minnie? Is there something I can do?" Manny blinked his big brown eyes.
"I don't know," Minnie paused and continued, "I've been thinking, it's getting late. Let's get a good night

sleep and meet here same time and place tomorrow. I need time to think. Maybe we can discuss it then. You need to get back to land, and I need to get back to the Crystal Cave."

With that, Minnie kissed Manny on his smooth forehead and dove into the water with a splash. In an instant she disappeared below. Manny stood there for a moment and wondered what was going on. What did she mean? Is Minnie unhappy or simply unfulfilled? I guess it'll have to wait until tomorrow. Manny stood up, flapped his wings once and rose into the sky. All the way home, he remembered only her kiss, and dreamed.

12

Manny made it home in time to watch the last seven innings of the local baseball game. One of his buddies saw him fly in and came over with a twelve pack to watch the big screen with Manny. All during the game Manny was remembering the sweet hours he spent with Minnie. He was lost in his day and couldn't concentrate on the game. His buddy Squawk asked a lot of questions while they were sharing their brew. "What's it like to be a bird and have a Mermaid girlfriend? How do you plan on starting a family if this gets serious?" Manny was at a loss for an answer. "I dunno." His head was spinning. He had no answers for what the future might bring. All Manny knew was that something was going on in his stomach and it was clouding his thinking. He sought only to be with his friend Minnie. "Who cares if she's a Mermaid? So what? She's my friend, and, and I love her! There! I said it. Go tell the whole darn flock! MANNY LOVES MINNIE! I don't care what anyone says. That IS the truth, and THAT is how I feel!"

13

Minnie made it back to the Crystal Cave before dark. She settled into her little crevice and was about to go to sleep when the wise old manatee Floyd came lumbering into her space with a BIG splash. "How ya doin' little lady? How was your day? Didja see your gentleman Seagull today?" Minnie smiled at the big old white whiskered manatee.

"Yes, I did. He told me he's traveled all around the world and has seen so much. He's got a lot of miles on him and is so interesting to listen to. I learned a lot about him today and he seems to be down to earth and honest. This may sound strange, but I'm very fond of Manny. You should see those big brown eyes. I just melt when I look into them. I tried to tell him about me, but couldn't equal all his experience. It didn't matter though, because there's a lot I don't know or understand about being a Mermaid. I ran out of words and explanations trying to describe to Manny the rationale and life of a Mermaid. I wonder at times if our only purpose is to allure human men, and sit on rocks brushing our long hair as sailors pass by."

Floyd swiped his whiskers with a fin and drew in a little closer. "You know the legends Minnie," exclaimed the wise one. "Maybe it's time for me to have a heart to heart discussion with you about them," followed by a deep breath and watery burp. "Remember one basic fact. Manatees are the most enlightened creatures on earth. We are very large, have a huge brain capacity, and are ancient and experienced in the ways of life and living. Only the manatee *knows* and understands the meaning of our legends. Not all manatees have this wisdom. Only a few older ones like me are given insight. That being said, I want to tell you a story. It may be a riddle, but in the end you'll learn some serious lessons that I want you to follow even though you won't totally understand."

"Why me Floyd? I'm already confused. Why do you want to pass on serious information to me? I thought you said only manatees had the secrets to our legends. Now you want to share them with me? The last time I looked in a mirror I was a mermaid. I really don't understand."

"Okay. Fair enough. There is a reason, but first you must listen to understand." Minnie nodded. "Now, let me begin at the beginning. I mean the absolute beginning (sigh). When mother earth was created all the animals were given domain over land and sea is where I'll begin. There were no humans. These sentient human beings were made as the final flower of a great experiment. It is written that man was made in the image of a Superior Consciousness that we'll call The Architect. Their bodies house this image. The image is in fact the consciousness or spiritual essence that inhabits it, not a physical manifestation as so many believe. Over many millennia the Creative Entity noticed this particle of design called human was becoming more warlike, and abusing the power and aptitude given him. From the dawn of time until now, the human race has been a thorn in the side of our grand design. Humans have destroyed the world several times. They have polluted the waters and the air, and caused increased violence to be unleashed through unnatural causes. Humans never "understood" that peace and harmony are the reason for their existence. They have lived in harmony with virtually no part of their world. At some point, no one knows exactly when, our Universal Architect began to weave an intricate web to capture and change the behavior of humanoids through an introduction of a non-rational entity that was entirely preposterous. This non-rational entity would be endowed with a meaning and purpose that alters logical reason and resolves our ill-fated search for wisdom and enlightenment. This outrageous creation will be mostly lore, but in the end bear great prophesy! Humans will listen, because their eyes cannot believe a non-conventional creation transcending human comprehension and denying the evolutionary process of logical ontogeny which is analogous to their perceived reality. However, this revelation may not influence the masses completely, but instigate a more rational behavior to a position where it can be manageable, and furthermore reduce barbarism that has extensively infected our earth. We needed a link between our principles of origin to the perception of the human species. That link is the riddle of our legends. It's a link that defines a specific significance to those who witness it.

While this development was taking shape, we manatees were giving birth to far more little girls than boys. For some reason we were out of sync with the balance of nature. This is when a select few human spirits began to enter into our bodies instead of human bodies. After a while these little creatures lost their manatee attractiveness excepting the tail, and transformed into a new life form called "Mermaid." Mermaids are a pure race of manatee hybrids. No one knows how it happened, and no one knows completely what it means. Mermaids are the missing link and vessel that will give birth to a new generation of humans who understand the mysterious way of our Cosmos. The only coincidental event we can identify setting these changes in motion commenced sometime near earth's last major cataclysm."

Floyd gazed deeply into Minnie's supple eyes and continued. "Minnie, I think it's almost time to solve the riddle. This is why I'm sharing it with you. I believe you're the one who possesses the answer within you that will alter the collision course our world is now on. I feel it in my old bones."

Minnie was more puzzled. "I still don't understand. I'm falling in love with a seagull. What does that have to do with the human race? I face ridicule for this because I'm more interested in a bird than a human. How can I be a credible key to a great answer to this, this riddle? I think I need advice on how to deal with my predicament and what to do before I go too far."

"Mmmmmm, as I said earlier Minnie, I don't have all the answers. I don't know what's at the end of the road, and I can't cross bridges which haven't yet been built. This is a process. I can only advise you. We can walk the walk and stay the path, but where it leads is not ours to know. Answers will be provided as we need them. We cannot plan the outcome of our actions, only the process by which we act them out. My advice to you is simple. Listen carefully and heed. Watch for signs and put one fin in front of the other. Don't tangle them by anticipating the next step. Keep on moving in the direction you're moving. There's something more than we can understand happening here, and I believe you are doing the right thing. Don't be too rational. This limits your thinking. Be open and willing to learn and become something new. Give Manny a chance to be the happiness you see in him when you are together, but don't make your life a symphony based on a single motif. Remember, Manny may be the love of your life, but don't forget to love yourself. Remember your heritage, your family, the Crystal Universe and all those things that have made you who you are before Manny came along. Don't lose focus, and don't lose yourself. Transform into your own change, and you will find a happiness and joy you richly deserve. That is my advice."

Floyd dove into the reflecting waters and departed for now. Minnie knew she would encounter her friend again and his wisdom would be important to her future. She also knew she must prepare herself for *the magnificence of the uncertainty that lies ahead.*

14

The next morning, Manny was up with the sun. "Today, I'm excited," he said to himself. "My stomach is rolling, it's sunny and warm, and there's a warm light wind over the ocean leading to our meeting place."

Today, Manny decided to save energy and take wing to an extreme altitude and ride the outgoing air corridor to his destination. This meant he'd have a long climb up to about seven-thousand feet. He flew very high on many occasions in the past, and was confident of a smooth and less strenuous flight. Manny went out on his front perch, and as he was standing at the edge flapping his wings, noticed he was being watched. He stopped and looked around. Nearly every seagull along the coastline was gathered near his home. Some were perched on power lines. Others filled trees and roofs of nearby buildings. Every shrub and fence line was jammed with seagulls. When he looked around he was greeted with a loud slowly rhythmic chant. The high-pitched screeching unison din screamed one word GO! GO! GOOOOOH! GOOOOOH! GOOOOOOH! Manny had not seen a neighborhood spectacle like this since he was a chick. A convicted car windshield pooper was trying to move into the rural neighborhood Manny lived in. Manny witnessed the entire scene. The screeching grew every day until the poop bird moved from the neighborhood. "Now they are all gathered and screeching for me to GOOOOOH! "I suppose this is a protest because I'm seeing a Mermaid? My buddy who came over to watch the game last night must have spread the word." I suppose when I exclaimed he could tell the world that he did. Now I can expect ridicule and harassment from all my friends and neighbors." Nothing is worse than being harangued by thousands of seagulls. In society it's intriguing when one "strays" from the mainstream for about any reason, he or she usually winds up outcast and a target of public ridicule. I wonder if it's because those masses wish they could dare to be different too, or maybe they're jealous because I'm happy. I believe most naysayers don't understand boundaries they live within are imaginary according to their own pre-formed ideals! I always felt my unique experiences in life are largely due to the fact that I seek them out by being open minded. We are all born handicapped to some degree. Our parents teach us everything, how to fly and search for food, and so on. They not only teach us how to use our instincts, our parents or whoever raises us, transmits their set of values into us. We receive their memory! We most often become affiliated with their religious denominations and political parties. We spend the rest of our lives making our own memories, but rarely break completely free of those original conformities given to us by our early mentors. This is how we perpetuate behavior of our species. Since no seagull has EVER engaged in friendship with a Mermaid, it's unacceptable in the eyes of all other seagulls to be friendly across species lines. These beliefs result from a memory implanted in their poor bigoted heads, because there's no information from experience to measure morality, or no way to say what is right or wrong. The act becomes judged negatively because the "memory" statement of our species says we are exclusively linked socially and romantically solely to our own species! This is what we are taught. If we don't buy into accepted social behavior, we are outcast and considered a threat to our own Seagull kind. This is where I am now."

With those thoughts and sounds of protest fading in the distance, Manny flew out to sea, higher and higher until the noise faded away. A feeling of freedom's power in his mind gave him strength to go on. Temperate winds carried Manny closer to his destiny. As suddenly as he calmed, Manny spotted clouds forming quickly over a stretch of ocean where he was headed. He realized that Minnie might see the same storm clouds brewing and wonder if he was thinking about skipping his crossing today. The thought of not seeing Minnie was painful. If Manny stayed home he'd be subjected to more harassment and ridicule from his peers. They would judge him weak and fallen from grace. That was NOT about to happen! Manny took a deep breath and plunged more vigorously toward his eventual consequence. Abruptly he was disoriented. The last thing Manny remembered was a bright searing flash followed immediately by an intense stabbing pain in his head. He tumbled from the sky into the sea below. His world went dark.

15

In Minnie's world her consequences brought open-minded inquiry instead of scorn. Her Mermaid friends became curious at first though not critical. Questions ensued but weren't necessarily answered. In her heart she wondered if she and Manny were building a relationship which in the end might hurt them both.

Minnie and her entourage of Mermaids returned to their rendezvous oasis as the sun rose over the ocean and brought up dancing reflections from the rippling waves. The temperature was warm but not hot. Formations of clouds resembling an armada of ships crossing the ocean marched across the sky. Huge celestial sculptures of chiseled faces in the heavens reminded Minnie of her ancestors and protectors who must be watching over her and Manny. She wondered if they approved of their budding love. As time passed, Minnie began to wonder why Manny wasn't there. She spotted storm clouds brewing and began to worry a little. Up to now he always arrived before Minnie. What if Manny began to have second thoughts and was cutting his loses by not showing up? What if he had an accident? She remembered something her father once told her when she was worried about something she couldn't remember. Minnie began her lament with the words "what if." He interrupted her and said, "Those two words are the saddest words in the English language (unless you are a person of science). Avoid these useless mind games with yourself and you'll be a happier person with a much less cluttered mind."

Minnie returned to reality. She knew there was no way of communicating when they were not together. The only cell towers in the ocean were in the Crystal Cave. It was impossible to transmit a signal as far as the mainland. Minnie and Manny's entire relationship was based upon trust and believing in each other. She prayed Manny didn't have an accident, and prayed he wasn't running away. Seeking comfort, Minnie reflected on a story her mother told her long ago.

A mother Manatee named Sally (short for Salad Lady) was teaching her newborn baby to swim. Baby Buddy was really quite adorable. He was blessed with one blue eye and one brown. He loved to amble around and play with other young manatees like himself. He learned Mattie's (the Manatee) song and it became his first song, of course with a new name.

"I'm Buddy the Manatee.
I eat everything I see.
I travel near and far,
to find a salad bar;
And have a little lunch,
Crunch, Crunch, crunch crunch crunch!
I'm Buddy the Manatee."

He lived by those words and thought Mattie was the best cousin in the world. Buddy was a living breathing handful for his mother. One day they were swimming in the open ocean outside the Crystal Cave, and a VERY large white shark suddenly appeared. When the shark spotted the mother and child manatees, he whipped his gigantic tail around and proceeded to unleash a massive roar into the water bearing his razor sharp teeth in their direction, followed by **"THIS LOOKS LIKE LUNCH TO ME!"** Sally didn't know what to do. She wanted to swim away as fast as she could with her baby. Instead, she froze in horror as tiny Buddy swam between them and stopped a few feet from the Great White. He was curious and didn't sense danger. Buddy always believed his mother would protect him from danger. All three were momentarily suspended in the water. The shark began to flex his enormous fins as he prepared to pounce on the little one. Suddenly, from nowhere a seal swam into the picture, evaluated the situation and darted away. Immediately the shark sped off chasing the seal into the ocean void. When Sally's heart stopped pounding, she gathered her little one and retreated into the Crystal Cave shaken, but intact. Later Sally was telling her story to Floyd. Floyd affirmatively nodded all the way through. At the end, Sally said, "Floyd, you've always said there's a moral to every story. Is there a lesson I should learn from this? I'm still shaking." Floyd smiled, and put his fin up under his chin before he spoke. "Well Sally, when you face fear with innocence, peace and serenity in your heart, courage of thought and understanding of spirit, fear usually melts away. If you run from it as the seal did, it pursues you. The moral clearly demonstrates when fear knocks at your door and is answered with faith and calm, only the echo of the knock will be at the door to greet you. Remember to hold your head up high no matter what. Sooner or later every storm passes away." Minnie was remembering. "Eventually, the scheme of all things is revealed as time unfolds. The whereabouts of Manny will be revealed. I'll be here every day until he returns because I believe!"

16

Manny was struck by lightning. He took an indirect hit and plummeted nearly seven-thousand feet into the water. Because his bones are hollow and his wings fell limp spanning into the air current, he more or less glided into the water face up. Manny was completely out and appeared dead. The storm which followed the lightning washed tree limbs and debris into the ocean from the mainland, and Manny washed up on a palm branch meandering with the current. Three days he drifted. Some of the time he was semi-awake though delirious.   The ocean was calm and occasional splashes kept him on the verge of consciousness and cool in the sweltering sun. Intermittent clouds shielded out intense sunlight and heat. His body temperature was low but normal. Hypothermia did not onset because of a layer of feathers protecting his skin. Somehow, Manny was stabilized, yet very weak from hunger and shock. Finally, Manny floated along the shore line near a beach and came to rest as the tide receded. He was wet, disoriented, didn't remember who he was or what happened. His mind and body was completely waterlogged. Manny remained there several hours before being discovered by humans walking along the beach searching for shells. One of them, a little girl named Angelica, picked him up. Manny felt like he was being handled by an octopus with wormy wet tentacles and a fleshy little fat face. Yuk! He was grateful, however, because he had no energy and couldn't lift a wing to help himself. Manny believed his life was about to end, and he'd be eaten or tossed into a dumpster and emptied into a landfill somewhere where his bones would be picked clean by rats! Angelica wrapped Manny in a paper towel she retrieved from their picnic basket and presented her discovery to mom and dad. Mom jumped back and exclaimed, "GROSS! Where did you pick up a dead bird?" Angelica replied in an even confident tone, "I don't think he's dead mama." Dad came to the rescue and gently lifted the injured seagull to get a better look. "He looks alive to me. I wonder what happened. It appears he's suffered some kind of shock and isn't able to move. Maybe he's too weak, or maybe he hit something when he was flying and fell out of the sky. I've heard of instances where birds have been struck by skydivers in this area. There's a lot of activity such as parasailing too. Poor guy doesn't have any apparent trauma injuries or contusions. I guess he's lucky Angelica." He was picked up by the daughter of a Veterinary Doctor. "Let's get him back to the office and get some fluids in him."

Mom protested! "Hey! What about our day at the beach. Are you going to sacrifice our day for a stupid bird? Geezzzz. They're a million seagulls in the world, and I suppose you're gonna try to save 'em all at the expense of your family? These birds are nothing but disgusting scavengers. Why can't you just let it go? It'll probably die anyway. "

The good doctor Jack replied calmly. "Alisha (wife), how can you act this way? Don't you realize your behavior is a mirror that reflects your own image? What influence will your words have on your daughter? This is a life you're cursing here. A creature of nature! This poor bird could be some bird's son, husband or father. I'm blessed to be a doctor of Veterinary Medicine and I believe most things happen for a reason. I see storm clouds on the horizon and think we should wrap things up here and head back anyway. "

Manny felt uncomfortable on the trip to the doctor's office. He thought, "If only I had a voice. I want to tell the doctor what happened and maybe he could give me something to get me back on my feet. I need to get to Minnie before she thinks I've deserted her. Then again, maybe this is a Higher Authority's solution to the problem we have. Maybe I should die and get it over with. I know one thing. Whatever happens I have no control over the outcome."
This was the moment I discovered the meaning of acceptance. I always believed I could change the world. I was strong and vital. I had what I thought was courage. I believed I was

more than just another nasty seagull. I believed I was "different." So much of this was fantasy, and so much was not. The fantasy part was my total belief in my perceived personal omnipotence. In the reality part was my belief I was special. The major flaw was that I thought I was more special than my peers! I assumed I was in control and that providence was shaped by MY hand. Ha! Try that on now. I can't move. I'm weak, dehydrated, and totally dependent on humans who will probably boil my body, pluck my feathers, and slow cook me in a crock pot until I become seagull stew. Arrrrgh! Being in power is an illusion. It gives me a false sense of security. I look around and recognize everyone in this world is dependent on others sometime in their lives. Babies are dependent on their mother for nurturing, feeding, grooming and training. So many adults (humans) have conditions and illnesses which make them dependent on others. In my species only the fittest survive. With humanity there appears to be more compassion and understanding of the vital nature of each individual life. The oxymoron to me is the contradiction of how humans can be so compassionate to the needy on one hand, and on the other hand destroy themselves and others for ethnocentric and religious reasons or political beliefs. How does love turn to violence? I presume the solution is to understand the social nature of our existence and accept that at some point we'll inevitably NEED each other. Our individuality is secondary to the social needs of our existence. When

I'm in the predicament I'm in now, I need to learn to accept my fate because fighting it accomplishes nothing. Not being able to accept the unchangeable only causes frustration and anxiety. I can dream about my destiny, however, in reality I can do nothing. Nothing at all.

17

Minnie was getting increasingly worried as the time passed. Her family, friends and Floyd all supported her. Minnie told them she made a commitment and was going to believe in Manny's return no matter what or when. As each day passed Minnie suffered her loss. Her visions of Manny and dreams of their love were fading. Early on Minnie fantasized about Manny's return, though as time flickered away her fantasy disappeared into gloom. Anger came next. Was she set up? Maybe Manny has another bird brained female in his life. All sorts of thoughts spun around her mind like a whirling dervish. Drama eventually gave way to worry. Did something terrible happen to poor Manny? Did he collide with a jet engine on his way to see her? Is he injured and laying somewhere with no help or support? The frustrating part was that she couldn't help. It was time for her to consult her mentor, Floyd. As Minnie lamented, he appeared in her dreams. "Floyd, what am I supposed to do? Manny has fallen (or flown) off the face of the earth. I miss him desperately. How do I cope? I have so many feelings going through me now. I'm angry he's not with me. I'm sad because I don't know where he is or what's happened. I don't know if he left me, or if he's sick or even dead! I don't know what to feel because I'm clueless. Please help me Floyd?"

Floyd scratched his whiskers a little with his fin and furrowed his brow. "Minnie, this is an age old question for which exist numerous alternatives. Let's examine them and then decide what's best for you." She nodded. "Now Minnie, he disappeared when he was supposed to meet you and has not been seen anywhere near your meeting place. Is that correct?" Minnie nodded again. "How long has he been missing?" "Two days" she replied. "Well, in my opinion that's plenty of time for him to have accounted for himself. Let's try a pragmatic approach by breaking these developments down logically. He's either injured somewhere, dead, or left you for some reason. The last one is more subjective. This is to say, if he left he either can't face you, or there's been an emergency in his life he needed to attend to. We mustn't dismiss the unknown because it's all unknown. What CAN YOU do? Let's look closer. My experience has always been to take care of myself when I'm unable to control or foresee what's going on around me. It's especially true in relationships. This is easier said than done, but don't count on someone else for your happiness. Happiness is an inside job! To properly advise, understand and guide you, I need to put myself in your shoes. It's difficult because I'm not you. BUT, if I were in your situation, I'd begin by suffering. That's right! Suffer! Enjoy it.

Wallow in it and be utterly miserable. Permit your feelings to run amok with all the negative scenarios you can muster. When you are sick of being heartsick, take a deep breath and rid your mind of the chaos you've invented for yourself. Until you have suffered your little heart out and cried your tears into a river, you'll hold on. Let it all out and begin to let go. Experience the pain! Enjoy it! There's no comfort in pain, only hardship. When you have finished and can suffer no more, necessity will cause change. Then it's time to search for rational answers. Quiet your mind and meditate. Center yourself. You will soon discover a Universe you never knew existed. The path of suffering sometimes can lead to a path of healing. Without suffering, we never know otherwise. The colors we see with our eyes are flat and one-dimensional without the colors in our hearts to bring them alive. When you light up your life with something more than someone else, you can discover greater meaning within. Self-discovery will heal you if you let it. After mourning, a new day will dawn. Learn to take a lesson from any trial you endure. Reality turns out to be focused when you open your heart to the healing powers of nature. I don't know what the answer is, but somehow the process of enlightenment and reality eventually merge. Give inner-peace a chance. The best advice I can give you Minnie is to remember life is about what you believe. For me it's a belief in the wisdom of my heart and hope. With those words, Minnie awoke from her dream. She decided to suffer a while longer by waiting. Every day Minnie swam to the "rock" and kept a watch in the sky. Every bird she spotted brought hope, and when they passed over sadness rushed in.

18

In the meantime, Manny was being nursed back to health by his human friends. The young girl who picked him up on the beach took particular care. Her parents, especially her father understood though they didn't particularly approve of her bringing a dirty, sick and nasty seagull home to nurse. Manny was given his own space. Angelica fed him with an eyedropper filled with some sort of liquefied bird food the Vet (dad) gave her. Slowly, Manny began to regain strength. He stood up after about two days but felt a little dizzy and disoriented. He teetered precariously on his perch, and any memory of his past was dull at best. Everything seemed to be a blur. He was living in a fog. Manny was aware of his identity, however, details of his recent history were run together and appeared disconnected. He kept dreaming about a mermaid which didn't make sense. Then the dream vanished and he heard voices of other seagulls chanting...Go...! Go...! Go...! His motor skills were so weak he finally collapsed fell off his perch.

As time progressed the dizziness finally wore off and Manny began to flap his wings once in a while. The vision of a beautiful mermaid and hallucinating voices chanting "GO!" continued to pound in his head. It took about six weeks for Manny to physically recover his bodily functions and balance.

As those days and hours slowly passed, Manny began to feel better each day. He exercised by hopping around the several perches in his large cage. Suddenly his memory was completely restored. Manny stopped in his tracks. For a few moments he wondered what happened. Then he remembered the lightning strike over the ocean. He remembered his fall, and recalled where he was going. "Oh Gosh! How long have I been out? Minnie's gonna leave me forever. I need to get outta here NOW!"

About that time, Angelica's father was walking toward the cage holding her hand and explaining how well "the seagull" was recovering. Manny heard the distinct words "he needs to be returned to the wild." He was relieved and filled with anticipation at the same time. Angelica didn't want to let go. Dad picked up the cage and carried it to the back patio. Manny noticed a cat sleeping on top of the fence where he needed to launch in order to fly away. Big crocodile tears streamed down Angelica's cheeks when she opened the cage door. Manny bounded out quickly and flew straight up to avoid the cat. Of course, Mr. Cat tried to rear up on his hind paws and swat him out of the sky. He missed and tumbled off the fence. Manny was tempted to make another pass over him and deposit some whitewash in his eye, but kept on moving. As he flew away, thankful for this wonderful family which had taken him in, he swore he heard Angelica's voice as he was going over the trees. She was saying, "Take care Manny, and travel well."

From then on, Manny supposed his rescue was divine providence, and Angelica was placed in his life at a specific time and place for that purpose. He realized this because she never heard or knew his name. Manny couldn't speak human sounds. When he heard her exclaim "Manny" he realized another invisible hand was caring for him, and was resolved more than ever now to return to Minnie. He believed something big was about to take place, and wanted to fulfill his part whatever it may be.

19

Though it was mid-day, Manny headed directly out to sea. This time he checked the weather forecast before he left. There were no seagulls gathered to taunt him. By now they must have thought he left the area. Manny's apartment was probably ransacked and torn apart. His belongings including his brand new computer and widescreen were probably taken too. Manny didn't bother to check it out because he had more important things on his mind presently. He flew toward the sun and never looked back. The upper airstream sped him along. He calculated his arrival to be well before sunset. Manny hoped Minnie's beautiful hair was dancing in the sunbeams and she'd be there to greet him with open arms. At the same time, he was worried she might think he deserted her and never wanted to see or speak to him again.

20

Meanwhile, one of Manny's Seagull "friends," his dark buddy named "Squawk," paid a visit to Minnie. He described to her what happened and warned her to stay away from Manny should he return. He said that no Mermaid and Seagull should be together. It WILL NOT WORK! Cross species relationships were doomed because of their "differences." He tried to reason with Minnie. He even told Minnie that Manny might never come back and that Manny had been approached by his peers before he left. He described the humiliation he was put through by his chanting friends and wanted her to know Manny was shaken and despondent. Chances are he was humiliated into submission and left without showing his face. More than likely he's imposed a self-inflicted exile out of personal shame and heartbreak. Minnie quietly reflected, waited and hoped for Manny's return. She kept her thoughts to herself. Little did Squawk realize Manny was already on his way. Minnie didn't take Squawk's squawking seriously. She acknowledged Squawk with a half smirk and dismissed him. Her vigil was unbroken.

21

Far above the meeting place there was a speck that caused a fleeting shadow where Minnie was sitting as he passed between her and the sun. Everyone looked up immediately. It appeared to be a bird circling almost in orbit. Minnie sat up and placed her hands above her eyes to shade the direct sunlight. Squawk, who had remained after he was dismissed and continued his never ending babble, flew up immediately and sped away out to sea. The Manatees and Mermaids attending Minnie all dove into the ocean and disappeared into the depths. Minnie was alone. Manny circled ever closer. History was about to be made. With a sudden bound the slowly circling seagull dove with blinding speed. About one hundred feet above the rock Manny appeared to stop in mid air. He glided directly toward the rock where Minnie was waiting. She held out her arms, scooped Manny up and hugged him with all the love in her heart. Both broke into tears. No words were spoken. The center of the world was in that moment and their love outshined the sun in the sky. As they embraced, a stunning aura formed and reflected into the vast darkness of space. It lit up as if the brilliance of the Aurora Barillas had suddenly burst into full splendor over the entire planet. Manny the Seagull and Minnie the Mermaid were together again at last.

II. THE JOURNEY BEGINS

22

After Minnie almost smothered Manny with her hugs, and nearly drowned him with kisses a long silence ensued as they stood in the sunbeams overlooking the flickering waters surrounding them.

Minnie broke the silence. "I don't know what happened and it really doesn't matter because I always believed you would return Manny." Manny smiled and looked down at the rock with an "ah shucks" look. He raised his head and cleared his throat.

"Minnie, I don't know where to begin. I was on the way to see you. Perhaps I wasn't as alert as usual and didn't see the storm clouds forming. I was chastised by the entire Seagull Nation. They wanted to expel me from their "clan" and exile me from the community. The local gulls gathered everywhere and chanted for me to GOOOOH! I was surprised and disappointed. I never realized the ignorance of my species. I always believed we are all God's creatures no matter what. We came from different places and look different for the reason we are of different species. SO WHAT! My parents always taught me life is about love." If this is true, I must have been created in the image of love. Therefore, if I love you, I'm merely expressing the love born in me. I know deep down the ignorance of others makes no difference. I believe there are greater reasons, exactly like those spoken by your legends, waiting to be fulfilled. I believe we're somehow a part of some sort of greater wisdom waiting for the right moment in time to be brought to light. I have no idea what plan is in store for us. I need to be able to "stand without knowing," and am certain what I do today will come about as my dream for tomorrow. When tomorrow arrives it's my memory and I want each memory to be filled first with power from a will stronger and loftier than mine, and then with fond recollections I have created for myself by the way I spend today. Minnie, I love you no matter what. I don't care if I'm a crappy old seagull."

Minnie's brow raised a little and broke into a beautiful smile. "Manny, we go far beyond the moment. I believe in my heart there's more to "us" than today. I believe in an unfulfilled destiny we share as we travel this road and walk through our veil of tears. Are we big enough to go for it? Can we shoot for the moon and if we miss, land somewhere amongst the stars? Are we strong enough to live a providence which will modify history as we know it? I believe the recent events in our lives were a test. I also believe we passed. Are we ready for the next step? Are we ready to march into the future with our heads held high and experience with enthusiasm the course of meeting fate eye to eye? I'm ready Manny, because I love you too for all the reasons you have given and more. We can from this moment forward join wing in hand and face our lives together as one."

And so they became.

23

Floyd was waiting in the wings. As Manny and Minnie sealed their commitment to each other with a kiss, he rose from beneath the surface with a splash. "Hi! I see you two finally decided to do the right thing." Manny looked at Floyd with a little scorn for interrupting their special moment. Minnie caught the glance and smiled as she placed her soft hand on Manny's head. "I thought you might show up pretty soon. Are you here to facilitate the commencement of our strange odyssey?"

"Yes I am," Floyd replied. "I'm at your service. Time has arrived for your fantastic voyage. Without hesitation, Manny spilled out the words, "When do we begin?"

Floyd, "Now."

No sooner did "now" fade from Floyd's lips when the world around them began to change. An eerie light blue glow reflected from the ocean surface. High in the heavens shone joie de vivre so bright all three had to shade their eyes.

Manny moved forward. "What's going on? I feel out of control and my head is spinning."

Floyd pondered then spoke. "Manny, you are confused because you're not in control anymore. Your lives are in the hands of a power greater than yours. From now on everything will have a different meaning. You're accustomed to understanding everything in black and white. What was once familiar is past." As Floyd spoke the firmament was changing colors until it transformed into one vast collage displaying every color and shade in the spectrum. The atmosphere seemed to pulsate in harmony as if it were connected to the heartbeat of a living creature. Manny held tight to Minnie's hand as they felt a "changing" in them as none they had ever known. The ocean rushed toward them like a giant tsunami. The waves became instantly gentle and embraced them with a surge that lifted into the heavens and rushed by their eyes like stars at warp speed streaking through the sky at night. Faster and faster they sped. Reality became a blur. Their velocity was so great they melded into pure energy brighter than before. Suddenly the sense of speed disappeared and dissolved. A feeling of serenity came over them as they discovered themselves inside an enormous celestial cathedral.

Bathed and dressed in purity, Minnie spoke her first words since the odyssey unfolded. "Manny, I know where we are. I know why we're here. I know why Floyd is here with us. I think I finally understand."

Manny was in awe. All he could do was gulp. His deep brown eyes darted in all directions. "Manny (he thought) you flew so high you reached heaven."

It appeared as though history was unfolding as in a movie or documentary of creation. Manny, Minnie and Floyd were moving backward through time. They were allowed to stay, or pause time as they willed and visit those special moments from their pasts. Minnie took them on a pass through the Crystal Cave to the origin and day of her birth. There they discovered a road leading into an unknown void wherein a new adventure materialized. Before them stretched a soft grassy road. Minnie's tail began to transform. She was able to glide over the grassy canopy with a beam of light which appeared to synchronize her movement

with her thoughts. The same thing
happened to Floyd. Manny became a
bit larger and more powerful. A gradual
change in them was taking place. Floyd
was the designated guide. He was
given a vision that explained the fortune
and purpose of their journey. Though
none of this made sense, Floyd
continued forward. "This way," he
exclaimed. Minnie and Manny followed.

24

 As Minnie, Manny and Floyd passed
through their flights of imagination
dreamlike visions replaced reality and
formed focused thought. In Manny's
dream he remembered his youth when
his mother was teaching him to fly. She
taught him to perceive with deeper
introspection, but neither dwell nor

obsess in a world removed from reality. Therefore, his awareness was acute and he believed by observing the minutest detail that nothing is as it seems. Everything is exactly what it is and can be stripped of pretense to the core when clearly apparent. "Now when I sail above the haze, I study the cloudy patterns and feel exhilarated for having arrived in a vast space above them. I become conscious of a spiritual correlation between what's below me and where I am at that moment when peace and tranquility slake every cell in my body. No clouds to block the sun and no turbulence will make my stomach churn. Everything below me is embedded in the proximity of the earth's gravity from whence I came. The earth and all its parts seem so low and far away. All the troubles and turmoil of the planet reside near its surface. By being above these vapors I can witness a special sort of harmony on a different plane. I suppose the point is that I need to pass through the conflagrations of my own existence to find peace, which is the eternal quest of every breathing creature. Only through trials and suffering do we find enlightenment. There's no way around it. Gotta suffer first. Then and only then am I prepared to understand why illumination emerges from beyond. Some of us never get there. Chaos becomes the sum of our discernment. This is the chance we take as inhabitants of a vast cosmos of random experience. We're robbed of our innocence and given an albatross which keeps us earthbound. We never see beyond our self-made fog. Peace is concealed in darkness and fear possesses us. Our wings are broken and inner-spirit mired in a blindness we suffer by the will of seagull-kind. All this results from inherited instincts, or comes to us in the name of a noble cause. In reality, it's a terrible excuse to tear apart our souls and feed them to the demons we call justice and common identity. In fact, it's a very real selfish pride and everyday prejudice given to us in massive doses of ethnocentric experience in our formative years. We are given memories that are better forgotten. I define these as ethics derived from the history of our past. It's such a shame to lose a soul that way. Beware of what lurks below. All I ever wanted was to be a sun ray that burns away the morning fog and lifts my spirit above the fray."

Manny awakened. He was standing on a beach facing an early sunrise or late sunset (not sure which). He had no sense of direction, whether facing east or west. Near him sat Minnie and Floyd. All three had dreamed.

Manny looked curiously at his traveling companions and painted his dream in graphic detail for them. "I suppose these dreams have something to do with where we're going. I tried to figure out what it meant for us. Initially, I felt it was a message to beware of the future. Then I realized it was a story of how I developed mistrust when I was a young bird. I sense my dream was a lesson for me not to mistrust what's unfolding. I'm being told I'm not in charge of the future. I need to believe in forces greater than myself and to them turn over my will to them. This dream was preparing me to accept the unknown."

Minnie listened intensely. "I had a dream too Manny. I dreamed I woke up and found I was washed up on a sand bar at low tide about a mile or so inland on a little river stream lined with a seawall. There were palm trees growing near the rivers' edge, a long concrete walk in the shade near the water, and a lot of luxury condos made of red brick with open patios behind a grassy carpet facing the water where I was stranded. A small pier jutted into the water near the walkway. Two pontoons, a small fishing boat and a catamaran were docked there. I was strictly an observer, and became concerned that I may be seen if people taking their morning walks happened to look in my direction. I needed to get back into the ocean because humans were not supposed to see Mermaids in this environment. They could catch me and put me in an aquarium somewhere as a freak of nature, or display me in a traveling circus. Before I was fully awake I felt uncomfortably alone and abandoned. No one came to my rescue. A small canoe was floating near me in the open water and I decided to jump in it when it grounded on the same sandbar I was on. After I "flopped" in, it pushed its way back into the water and began to float along in a slow current. I looked around inside and discovered a couple oars lying under some life jackets near the middle of the canoe. The sides of the canoe came up past my lower body. My "tail section" wasn't exposed to onlookers. However, my topless upper body was in plain sight. I quickly put on a life jacket to cover myself and looked like a happy little boater row, row, rowing my boat gently down the stream. In any case, I picked up the oars and decided to row myself back to the ocean. Rowing was easier said than done. I had never rowed anything before. When I stroked to the right the nose of the boat went to the left. When I stroked to the left it went to the right. When I tried to miss rocks and debris I wound up running head long into them. I couldn't avoid the smallest obstacle. It seemed as though the harder I rowed, the quicker I crashed. The stupid canoe overturned when I hit one big rock. I turned it upright and noticed I had a little audience on the bank when I received applause for my successful effort. In the next moment a bizarre twist to my plight occurred.

An old man came wading out into the current. I thought for a moment that he was walking on not in the water. The water never rose above his ankles. He waded his way directly to the canoe. I was so afraid because I couldn't hide what I am. He gawked but exhibited no surprise as he waded up beside me and peered in the canoe. "My name us Andy," he said. "I wasn't walking on the water in case you are wondering. I know where the rocks are," he smiled. "I see you're a bit "different" from the average damsel in distress. I presume you need someone to help you get back to the mouth of the river where it empties into the ocean?"

"I nodded because I needed help though I was a little scared."

"Well, I can help. I love to canoe," Andy said. "When I was younger I used to give my friends a little tour of our beautiful river. I often sat in the front (of the canoe) and went along for the ride, or sat in the rear to steer. I always liked to steer, but don't we all? Most of the time I rode in the stern and carried the burden of the entire boat."

Minnie mused. "Whenever he said something like that, it appeared he was looking right through me with a gentle knowing smile."

Andy continued. "In the beginning I liked to row as hard as I could. I liked to row fast. Anytime I encountered rapids or trouble in the water, I rowed like a mad man to stay clear. I learned that "fast" was not the answer. What always happened if I rowed fast in a current heading for a protruding rock? I enhanced the current and locked onto the rock like a runaway missile. I made it to the rock quicker and invariably crashed or swamped the boat in my futile efforts to veer out of the way. I watched you do the same thing young lady. I presume because you're a sea creature, you haven't had much experience with canoes. Now, if I tried to row through calm waters to speed up the trip, I accomplished nothing by the excursion's end excepting sore shoulders and fatigue. Most importantly, I was in the water and missed the trip. Do you know what I mean by that?"

Minnie looked at Floyd and shrugged. "I thought I knew what he meant but I didn't understand until I reflected on my own life, and pictured myself rowing down my stream of continuation struggling for control. I smashed into one rock after another."

Andy went on. "I want to explain something to you. By the way, what is your name little mermaid?"

"Minnie, I replied. I was still a bit recoiled and didn't know which way to turn. I sat completely tensed up and helpless."

"The lesson for me was to learn how to "scull," Andy explained. "Today I understand. The river has its own force of direction. That's something I can do nothing about. I can't change or control it. The river has its own obstacles. I can't remove those obstacles either. Because I'm on my own crossing, I need to do no more than a few simple things to get where I need to be. I learned how to scull to avoid fighting the surge. Sculling allows me to use it instead. If living is a type of movement across a continuum of time and I learn to scull, I'll get fewer bruises and dents. I point the boat a little by rowing backward. I "guide" it through rapids, not force it. I needed to learn to practice this principle in all my trips. I had to find a way to accept where it's leading, and trust its direction without fear. When I did this, I finally understood and lived my voyage with confidence, acute awareness and sharper perception. When rapids appear, scull. When obstacles appear, scull. It doesn't always work. There are times when so many obstacles appear in my path they seem unavoidable. I may have to get out of my canoe, get in the river and carry the canoe around the turmoil. That may be a little hard for a mermaid to accomplish. I need to learn to be creative and do whatever it takes. Laziness is not an option. I either make a decision to go through or around the rapids. When I make this decision, I stick to it with all the tenacity I can muster. I may slip on the mossy rocks and fall. I can't worry about events that have not occurred! I can't fret about whether the decision of my sculling direction was correct or a mistake. If I became apprehensive, I'd do little more than sit on the bank of life and watch the river go by. My passageway might end in my own conceived despair. Today I forge on. I accept the current. This doesn't indicate I should adapt to it. I don't want to imply that I pull in the ores and let its natural course cause me to crash into every obstacle in my way. This is what sculling is about, healthy acceptance. It is the ability to acknowledge there are obstacles to overcome, yet not adapt to the perceived fear of their presence and fall prey to unknown dangers. I have no control over turmoil that crosses my path. However, I alone choose which way to travel. The more I practice the choices I am given, the better I become in choosing my choices."

Andy continued. "There's also the act of believing the rapids will carry me to where I need to be according to the way I steer. I can learn to enjoy the water, trees, birds and a sun drenched world of personal whereabouts as I go through this gamut of linear travel. I won't row fast. Why should I want to live too quickly? I want to savor the nature I am one with. I want to learn to enjoy the feeling of animated rapids as I pass through them. Everything in nature has its particular purpose for being. As I experience the tides of time to their fullest, I become immersed in an ever-expanding universe that began in my own inner realm. Thus, I can know a richer and more meaningful way of life. Hope is the message Andy passed on to me. From that one word I understood his most important lesson. He apparently lived those lessons with joy and a smile I'll never forget. He taught me another lesson too. I was helpless and at his mercy. I considered it necessary to trust him and let go of my fear. Reaching out and asking for his help was all I needed to do. He obliged and climbed into the boat. With my fears vanquished, Andy guided us downstream. When we reached the ocean delta I bid him farewell and thanked him. Andy said to me, "Remember Minnie, when you feel helpless and alone try remaining at peace with the present. Turn over your will and your power to the forces of your creation. Lift your eyes upward, take a deep breath and be resolved."

"Wow!" Floyd added with a loud crunch as he munched on a carrot. "This was excellent. My dream was one about the future, and I suppose it deals with what was so vividly experienced in both your dreams. For some reason, as I mentioned before, I've been chosen as your guide and am to receive instructions about where we are going and how we're gonna get there. We've all been put on a mission which will likely change the course of time and fate of the world. We face a human race full of turmoil and danger. A world full of violence, war, pollution and of fears you so eloquently dreamed about. Our goal is not to change the will of man, but to offer alternatives. We were chosen to be involved in becoming a sort of liaison to a new era of enlightenment for humankind. If it works the planet can be saved from certain unnatural desolation. We can live happily ever after if we try. We know what happens when we don't listen. I remember the immortal words of our forefathers. "Faith believes in the wisdom of the heart and the reality of the rainbow." So we stand here on the threshold of providence. Before we take our first steps, we need to demonstrate our individual conviction." Floyd continued, "I want to ask both of you, and myself, to go to the water's edge where the tide meets the sand and recedes."

Manny, Minnie and Floyd all moved to the waters edge. Manny felt warm water lapping up over his feet. Minnie and Floyd felt water pass under their tails as it gently surged forward over the sand. Floyd described his message.

"I would like all of us to look out over the immense deep sea. Envision every detail. See the sun rising and note the blue sky with those cotton clouds. Observe rhythmic patterns from every wave and feel the warm sea waft as it rolls over your feet or tail. Relax. Close your eyes and empty your mind. Breathe naturally and regularly. Release tension in your shoulders and accept nature into your character. Hear the roaring ocean and gulls squawking. Taste the briny spray as it moves across the beach. Become one with this peaceful place."

Floyd waited. After several minutes he resumed. "Open your eyes slowly and remain fixed in your relaxation. Now turn your thoughts gradually to your life as it is and has been. From each memory, choose your troubles and one by one write them in the sand. Write them side by side, and in rows, but make sure they remain within the fingers of the tide. When finished, either stand or face the ocean, or sit in the sand and face the trickling waves as they caress your extremities. Close your eyes. Take a deep breath. Let the calm of creation consume you. Become a living entity within it. Be your feeling. Unleash your spirit. Turn out your pain and let the power of nature devour your troubles written in the sand. Open your eyes and observe as the tide washes up over what you have written and gently lifts it entirely from the beach. Finally, witness as those hands of water and spirit carry away your sadness into the sea. Let your spirit be free, as free as the wind that moves by mystical energy and invisible force. When we have given our burdens over, we will travel lighter and faster. Our passage to immortality will unfold before us. From what we are today a blossom shall open as we transform into to what we will be."

25

Immortality is a place beyond revelation. It's a concept and reality all in one. No one knows its boundaries or limitations. We wonder after some speculation why we don't understand what isn't. A byway to immortality is one that exists when an intelligent creature learns to accept the nuances of an unknown as reality, and is comfortable with fate as a primary guide and purpose for all things whether self-evident or only in thought. Manny, Minnie and Floyd were in this reality. A crossroads appeared consequent to their love of life. A new direction was chosen from which an alternate reality emerged and materialized with each tentative step. An inner-illumination guided them as these purified entities entered into an incredible realm of accepting without knowing any truth from this multi-faceted corridor they passed through. A song without lyrics sang to their spirits and provided melodic rhythm to their gate. It birthed within their bosoms a peace and resolve designed for a greater purpose over an infinite and all encompassing sphere. Each of these crusaders were becoming more than any of them could individually fathom. A vast door was opening as a new truth became crystal clear. Then and suddenly, an alteration to another phase arose from a luminous geometric design that burst open with blinding force and spectacular display of light.

26

A supernatural rift in time appeared. In its center a portrait overlooking multiple rising suns beaconed with molten tentacles. It formed an oval disturbance and cellular tremor which vacillated in reflections from the ocean. Manny went forward to meet it and became fused in the blink of an eye. He flew into its heart and was instantly blended into a new "future world" from the past. Slowly the earth turned. Manny felt a little nauseous as he tumbled with the tide of changing colors and bright stars forming streaks in the sky from tiny dots. Traveling forward in reverse, Manny began to see the history of the earth rapidly unfold again as time sped backward faster than before. He felt like he was in a three dimensional movie. Manny was living through great events in history. He looked into the eyes of Gandhi. His Spirit was being distorted far beyond routine seagull dynamism. He was beginning to understand nature, and enlightenment was replacing suffering. Manny focused inwardly. He was being reborn. Everything sped as fast as light could travel. It felt like a gigantic blast from the finale to a fireworks demonstration. Finally, Manny floated in a white light to the ocean once more and was quietly carried to what appeared to be a peaceful exotic island. The sky was red, and the optics in the heavens made it appear the time of day was near sunset, yet there were two distinct spheres brightly lighting the fire sky and forming a concentric image. Manny rose to his feet on the cool sandy beach where he was deposited. He shook off the water and walked up the coastline. There was a cool zephyr to soothe his strong and uncommonly erect stature. Manny breathed in wholesome and fresh smelling salt air. As he made his way along the shoreline he discovered he was in a different world altogether, and probably in a different time. There were huge tracks which no doubt belonged to

large mastodons and dinosaurs. Other
birds he spotted resembled the giant
Pterodactyls he learned about in his Pre-
Historic Reptilian Bird studies in High Fly
School. Manny also noticed the earth
was unstable. In the distance he could
see and hear massive volcanoes
thundering their eruptive threats as if
this were a very young planet in its
formative age. His next observation
was the absence of humans. Manny
looked around nervously. "I guess I
really did it this time. I had to fly into
that infernal portal. I suppose I'm on
an expedition through time. I hope I'll
see Minnie again someday." Naked
realism was replaced by stomach
nausea. "There may be no way out."

27

Floyd and Minnie stood speechless on the breach. Floyd shook his head. "I wish Manny would have waited a little longer before flying into that chasm. I had a few things to share with you both. I wanted to fill you both in on the reason for this adventure. It'll have to wait now until we're all united in the "New World." Minnie, I think we both need to follow him in there now and hope we end up in the same place on the other side. Time is of the essence. I don't want Manny to get too far into the vision without us."

Minnie was puzzled. "What do we do? Can't you tell me what the big secret is and maybe I can think of something to help?"

Floyd replied. "There isn't time. We need to move in now. Come on Minnie, let's go."

Floyd nudged Minnie toward the portal and she was sucked in quickly.

28

Minnie was whisked into a fantasy similar to Manny's. Her world was turned on its side. She began to lose reference to her orientation, floated, spun, sped and then slowed to envision the history of her heritage. Minnie traveled through a mystical crystal cave. She witnessed its near destruction and followed its path to its very origin. She looked upon the faces of ancient and wise ancestors of her world. The great god Neptune materialized in her mind. History was traveling backward as she became a participating bystander to the times and events of conception. At last, Minnie slowly glided on a light beam toward another world. She was far above the ocean, and mused that this is what it must be like to fly. Minnie felt an overwhelming serenity, fear and resolve all at once. She arrived in a land unlike any she had ever known. Minnie found herself in a garden full of astonishing fruit bearing trees and voluptuous bushes. Everything living possessed an odd inner peace. As far as she could see, the landscape was a dreamlike painting disappearing into an invisible infinity on a road leading to the great unknown. She was placed on a smooth flat rock in the center of a stream rippling over rocks. It was so clean the water was pure, cool and blue. There was no evil lurking beneath. Her rock was lined with a velvety moss which added to her feeling of comfort and softness. A light wind passed through the trees and caressed her hair. Pictured within this paradise was a visual rendering so peaceful, no master artist could create a work of art to represent the absolute quiet harmony of these moments. Minnie could see what appeared to be two suns and decided it was an optical illusion because the warm atmosphere waved over the horizon and created a mirage like effect from heat generated by distant volcanoes. Minnie felt alone. She remembered the assurances of Floyd and took a deep relieved breath. "Everything is inevitable," she spoke aloud. ""When I am supposed to understand, I will. I hope." Minnie fixed her eyes upward as if seeking an answer. A tear slowly rolled down her cheek. Her eyes were glassy as she spoke again. "I'm grateful for the amazing life breathed into me, and thankful for being chosen to fulfill the ancient legends. Whatever is my noble purpose, I pray it be with Manny by my side." With that she sobbed softly. Her tears ran into the water and trickled downstream into the loveliness surrounding her countenance. A poem came to mind her mother sang shortly after she "changed" into a mermaid. They were words of a Sara Teasdale poem entitled "Coins."

Life has loveliness to sell
all beautiful and splendored things.
Blue waves whitened on a cliff,
soaring fire that sways and sings;
and children's faces looking up
holding wonder like a cup.

Life has loveliness to sell
music like a curve of gold.
Scent of pine trees in the rain,
eyes that love you arms that hold;
and for your Spirit's still delight
Holy thoughts that star the night.

Spend all you have for loveliness,
buy it and never count the cost.
For one white singing hour of peace,
count many-a-year of strife well lost;
and for one breath of ecstasy,
give all you have been or could be.

From her reminiscence, Minnie found
tranquility, silence and resolve.

29

As soon as Minnie entered the portal,
Floyd waited long enough for her to be
swept into the time warp when he
bravely moved his massive self inward.

Floyd suddenly felt very light. He had the sensation of flying. His adventure traversed a parallel between the crystal cave and human history. At this juncture he realized they were connected, as he always thought. Floyd knew this was a time when the sequence and resolution of those ancient prophecies might be revealed. No longer was a peaceful little world within the crystal cave there to protect him. Bold reality waited. Its sensation wasn't foreboding, but more of a contemplation of past contravention, replaced by an omnipotent hand and a feeling of calm fleeting from notion. It felt more intuitive because deep within he realized his heart knew what was true more than his mind believed what it was taught. Floyd underwent a humble spiritual awakening. As times gone by unfolded the future revealed itself with clarity. Floyd's eyes were wide as clarification penetrated his wits. He blazed with such brightness, luminance escaped every pore of his body and brought visibility to where none was known here-to-for. At last Floyd blossomed into ecstasy. From happiness his flame increased and his expression was more bravura than his wildest dream. Floyd had found Dharma! The past became an elucidation of the future, and his visions turned into prophecies borne from the rim of infinity. Floyd, this simple Manatee, knew more than all the great initiates born to humanity. His knowledge and learning had always been vast, now dwarfed by a deeper wisdom burned into a new and living reality; a reality superseding everything alleged to be real.

30

Floyd awakened from his sojourn. He found himself at the foot of a large rock in the midst of a rippling brook. He saw and heard exotic birds and water trickling into the pond where he arrived. The world he entered was primal and beautiful beyond description. As he surveyed his new environment, he slowly turned around and peered directly into the sunlight. Floyd visualized a reflection in the water and a ghostly shadow on the protruding rocks. It came into focus.

Minnie was amusingly watching as Floyd inspected his surroundings. "You made it Floyd. This is such a strange place.

It's beautiful despite the fact that it's kind of wild. It appears to be exotic and uncomplicated. Where are we Floyd? Where's Manny?"

Floyd gathered himself. "Well, little lady, I think we're in The Garden of Ed..." and then he was interrupted by familiar flapping sounds of Manny making his grand entrance as he swooped down from the sky. He gingerly landed as close to Minnie as he could. She scooped him up in her arms and kissed his soft head and beak. "Manny, we all made it. Where have you been?"

With a sheepish smirk he cleared his throat and flippantly retorted, "Certainly not painting Hoover Dam." They all laughed. Minnie continued, "Manny, I was about to ask Floyd what's going on and where are we when you arrived.

Floyd, can you tell us now what's going
on?"

"I can Minnie, but it wouldn't make
much sense at this point. However, I'll
tell you where we are, what we're here
to do and help guide you through each
threshold as they open. First of all, we
have arrived in the beginning. I mean
to say this place is Eden. The earth is
very young. We have traveled a very
long way back in time."

"Why?" Manny blurted out.

Floyd calmly responded, "Seagulls are
all impatient to a degree. I'll tell you.
The two of you have been chosen to
deliver the world the second greatest
creation in all of history. You remember
how troubled our future world has
become? Pollution, wars, famine, mass
hysteria, economic collapse, and
worldwide cataclysms are everyday

events. The poles are melting, brothers are pitted against brothers, fierce storms, tsunamis and severe weather everywhere shakes the earth's crust and destabilizes the planet. Bleakness surrounds us. The world is in its "end time." We, that is you and Minnie, have been given a special mission by a Higher Authority to change it all by delivering tidings to mankind which may save their world. I was given a vision to see your future unfold and understand what it is that you and Minnie will bring into the world. We'll experience it together. I will help you. Both of you need to stay focused. Keep your minds open, your hearts light and your love stronger than ever and you will see this through."

Manny replied again. "Floyd, you said a couple of words I'd like you to elaborate. You mentioned there were to be tidings delivered to the human race that *may* save them. Is this some sort of experiment or what? Is there anything we can do to help our future world? I love Minnie and Minnie loves me." Minnie smiled sheepishly. "How can we, a Mermaid and a Seagull, affect anything relating to mankind? Most people don't even believe in mermaids and who would ever believe in a talking seagull?"

Floyd furled his whiskers, "Believing is the key Manny. Your love is like none other since the beginning of time. You and Minnie are here to fulfill an ancient prophesy. None of us completely understand it yet. I was given a vision to witness on a grand scale. Your mission is solemn, it's serious, and is superlative beyond perception. You are living an impossible dream and are under special protection. You need to believe in order to survive. What I meant by the word "may" is that mankind will have a similar mandate. However, humanity also has a free will to reject or accept the reality of what is about to happen. They can choose to believe and change, ignore and doubt, or simply reject power that is being given to save them. You will open new pathways in a new world. Humanity will either walk with them or be so obsessed by a profound past rhetoric of misshapen logic that these new ways might easily disappear into mysterious dark shadows cast by those already gone.   Who wins? No one knows. Not even those who are above the stars!"

31

Floyd continued. "Have either of you ever wanted things to be different in our future world? Can you feed hungry children, heal the sick and comfort broken spirits? Did you ever dream of a world without war and envision people living in harmony with themselves and each other? Do you believe you can be a part of the change you dream of? Throughout history many sentient beings have made a difference and many died trying. Believe in yourself and have faith in a greater purpose! Faith is defined as *"The substance of things hoped for and the evidence of things unseen."* Never forget this. The origin of this verse is from "Hebrews" 11:1. Is it a coincidence that numerology places significance on certain numbers and interprets them within their reference by location? Eleven (11) is a reference to the end and judgment of mankind and one (1) is a reference to the beginning. Is there a message here for us? What does it tell us? When doubt spawns fear can we stay on course if we believe? If faith is the belief in what we hope for, maybe the evidence of things before unseen can clarify meaning in that which we never previously understood. For me it's easy to see. From the end (11) we discover the beginning (1) when we trust the message of this simple verse. Carry these thoughts with you to the end of your dream and you can transform the history of future generations yet unborn. Be steadfast in what you believe and truth will be revealed." Floyd added, "Shall we continue?"

Floyd motioned his front fin toward the east where the sun rises and the entire landscape began to rapidly move. The scene magically changed into a vast ocean. The force of change moved them into shallow waters. Tranquil balmy waves caressed their feet and tails. As the background settled they were positioned directly in front of a large rising sun. It almost felt like it could be touched if they reached out. Gradually it morphed into a gigantic ball of fire. Within the sphere appeared a reflection of Manny, Minnie and Floyd. Finally, a magnificent constellation of colors ascended like the great Phoenix from the ocean. Floyd moved a little toward them in the sand as his massive

manatee body would permit.
"Children," he spoke. "The time has come. The all Seeing Eye is on us now. This is symbolic of that eye which guides the universe and under whose watchful care the stars and planets perform their astonishing revolutions. In this moment it pervades the innermost recesses of your hearts as you become one within it. Both of you are being re-formed into a new image." Again Floyd waved his fin as an amber light blazed from both Manny and Minnie like a colossal golden aura. The fulfillment of the ancient prophesies had been set in motion.

32

A metamorphosis of physical conversion supernaturally unfolded. Slowly Minnie changed first because hers was the easiest. Her Mermaid tail felt warm and soft as it flushed brighter than her outer light. The split fin at the end began to draw out as her bodily scales dropped to the ground. Minnie's torso also altered as her elongated tail stretched into two human legs. Her whole lower body distorted slowly until she was completely humanized. Minnie's beauty was radiant and intact. She could arguably be seen as the most beautiful human in the universe. Minnie was perfect! Her long flowing hair and beautiful physique, faultless posture, and absolute proportion was beyond belief.

Manny and Floyd looked on in awe. "What is going on Minnie? Are you okay?"

She nodded to him, pointing at her new lower body. "Manny. Look at yourself." His eyes focused on his own reflection in a clear pool of water beneath his feet. "I don't understand," he called out.

Manny was becoming another creature altogether. His wings were changing into human arms, and his reptilian feet were changing into human feet and legs. His entire body was reforming and growing from his head through his spine down through his trail. He was glowing with a feeling of warmth and great strength seeping into his pores. Manny's beak turned into lips and formed a mouth. His nostrils formed a nose and his entire appearance changed as his pointed face became human. His eyes were still those big brown eyes

Minnie fell in love with. Manny took in a very deep breath to expand his new lungs and when he exhaled his feathers fell to the earth next to the shed scales from Minnie's tail. Manny was as perfect as Minnie. His body was molded and rippled with muscles that seemed to flex with a robust strength whenever he moved. Minnie and Manny rose to their feet together as human beings. Looking with love into each other's eyes, they embraced. The magnificent eye in the sky appeared as a rising sun illuminated the joy of the moment. The universe had revealed its life force. Manny, Minnie and Floyd knew it was The Great Architect who guided them and chose the moment they fell in love to bestow their extraordinary fate.

33

Floyd remained a Manatee. Minnie and
Manny were transformed, but
genetically Minnie was a Mermaid and
Manny remained a Sea Gull. Floyd knew
his part of the journey was nearly
complete and soon he must return to
the future from whence he came.
Floyd made his way to the foot of the
large boulder where Manny and Minnie
were standing. "Time has come for me
to go back to our origin in the future.
The two of you will remain here under
the watchful protection of the Great
Spirit. He will guide you through the
rest of your voyage."

Minnie objected. "Floyd, why can't you
stay a little longer? Why do you have to
go? There's so much more to be done

and we want you here to see us through."

"Minnie. I already know the outcome. It's written in our legends."

"Then please stay Floyd!"

Manny intervened. "I can't pretend to understand what's going on here, but I do know there has to be a reason for what Floyd's doing. I hoped you'd be with us all the way too Floyd, but I understand if you say you must go. I wish there was a way we could communicate with each other across time when we need your wisdom, uh, or at least want to know if the Yankees made it to the World Series. I suppose all we can do is wish you well. It almost feels like you are dying and we will never see or hear your voice again. I wish I knew why. I wish you could stay, but I suppose we can only accept fate as it directs our lives. Isn't that what is called living life on life's terms?"

Floyd responded. "It's a little like dying I suppose. But you realize only bodies die. Relationships don't. What we've shared we'll always have. In reality, I haven't been born yet. The only change is our perspective. You see today *and* in the past. I spoke and you listened. Now you can speak. Think of me as the one who is listening. When I return to the future, I'll be sitting at the feet of your ancestors one day, and then I will be your student. You see, faith believes in the wisdom of the heart and the reality of the rainbow. We came here on a rainbow. Our hearts have guided us to this place so far, and the insight you are given in the days ahead will see you through. Never forget this. Always be open minded to new ideas, otherwise you will never find truth. *Believe in* the wisdom of your hearts and listen to your still small voice within. The veracity of your dreams will bring into focus all those things unseen and hope will make them real. I'll stay for your wedding and then I must go. After all Manny, you'll need a Best Man."

34

Floyd immediately became enveloped in a glittering mist of blue tinted ice-crystals. His body transformed into a tall older human male with a wise and gentle face adorned with a white flowing beard. "This is only temporary my friends. I'll revert to my former jolly manatee self when this is over. No one will believe who I am or recognize me if I go back home like this," he laughed.

35

Manny was contemplating what was happening around him. As many "Grooms" experience, he felt a little uneasy. How can a Sea Gull and Mermaid become man and wife? How do we explain this to our children? What will they look like? Are my feet getting cold?

"I'm confused Floyd. How's this gonna work? I'm afraid I'm being swallowed by something so vast I don't seem to comprehend what's really going on. Am I losing it? You know I love Minnie but this is beginning to feel too tough for a simple seagull like me to grasp."

Floyd finally realized why he was needed to council his friends. "Manny remember you're no longer a seagull. Your mind understands what you have been taught; your heart, what is true. Open your mind and your heart. If you can't seem to understand, then believe! Remember our mantra. Faith believes in the wisdom of the heart, so listen to your heart. Now it's time for you to believe in yourself. What you don't understand doesn't make it less real. If your mind isn't open to new ideas and experiences and you refuse to climb out of your cocoon, you'll never experience the true quintessence of life. Even more, you'll never know the truth. You think this is hard? So what? Don't miss out on the greatest moment of your life because it's hard to do or understand. Embrace change. Accept the change you are and live life with fête. Celebrate the new Manny. Listen to the fanfare as it rises and trumpets your calling. Firmly take hold of today and measure your time by the multitude of happiness and love you have grown to be."

36

All three of them climbed on the flat rock in the stream. The rock began to rise. As it rose, Minnie radiated in a milky glow. She was becoming transformed into a beautiful bride with a long flowing white gown, and the ringlets of her hair sparkled in the sunlight as her entire being became a breathtaking countenance to be beheld as the most perfect woman in creation. Manny was undergoing a spectacular change of his own. He was now dressed in a handsome tuxedo. His chiseled features and clean shaven face were as clear and clean as the bluest waters in a calm ocean. His hair was as perfect as Minnie's, and the caress of a gentle breeze gave life to his magnificent stature. All three stood in a bright sunburst. All three arose into the clouds upon this island of tropical paradise that could only be compared to the fabled garden they came from. This is the Eden where dreams are born and the cradle of creation.

Upon the clouds were other floating islands. Each was populated by all the creatures on earth. The event was grand! One could hear the Herald

Trumpets announcing a grand entrance. Minnie began her walk through the mist arm in arm with Floyd. A multihued flame appeared over head as they approached the altar where Manny waited tall and proud. The wedding march was announced by another fanfare, and a deep low reverberation from the giant celestial pipe organ began the procession.

Minnie arrived at the blissful altar where Floyd presented her to Manny. They both stood facing an adornment of white orchids and cal lilies. Under the highest arch of a blazing aurora they stood bathed in sunlight. A deep iridescent blue light formed in front of the altar. Standing before them in human form was a simple dove named Buddha. Buddha faced Manny and

Minnie and softly recited their sacred vows.   During this time, another conversion transpired. Clouds formed into floating cherubs. The sun became a colorful array of spotlights that reflected little beams which glistened like water droplets in a stream during a rain shower.   Every detail of those moments was as perfect as paradise could fathom. Manny and Minnie became man and wife that fateful day. Together, they would change the world.

37

As the festivities after the big event continued, Floyd prepared himself for his trip back to the twenty-first century. "Life won't be the same without Minnie and Manny," he thought. "How do I say goodbye? Goodbye is a contraction that means God be with you. I understand these two special mortals are protected by legends, but how am I going to leave knowing my best and dearest friends are separated from me by more than two-thousand years? I'll never forget these days and our voyage into the unknown. I can only hope the world will comprehend what we have done here today as a good omen for our fragile future world. I am and always will be a simple Manatee. I'll swim in the ocean and hope I'm not run over by a speed boat. I trust Manny and Minnie will remember all we shared, and understand our bond of friendship will always live between us as long as we never forget where we came from, and what we have accomplished was for a much greater purpose. Our connection will survive time and distance. Deep

within our hearts a sacred place will
dwell where special memories are never
forgotten. Now it's time to go.

Floyd returned to the party and greeted
the guests. Amusingly, Floyd noticed a
few other manatees. He was pleased
none of them recognized him in
"human" form. What a party it was!
Can you imagine a party in outer space?
No amenity was left out and no detail
was too small! Manny felt very much at
home because the reception resembled
a restaurant he visited in Vegas. No
humans attended, excepting of course,
the recently transformed Manatee,
Mermaid and Sea Gull. The reception
was definitely open air. It was perched
on a very large cloud surrounded by
thousands of smaller ones. Each had
their own table and white linen, wine

glasses and pure golden silverware. The china was the finest quality in the universe. It had a sort of aqua iridescence and reflected an unusual clover like pattern. The cake was magnificent. There was enough to feed the thousands of guests in attendance. It stood over twelve feet high. The icing was white with ornate blue scroll trim and adorned with real roses, daises and a variety of colorful flora garnished with greenery made from the icing. An ice sculpture depicting a mermaid looking upward with a Sea Gull sitting on her arm looking into her eyes stood in a fountain of punch. It was symbolic of the occasion and represented a mystical union and reality that love conquers all. The waiters were beautifully attired penguins. They wore their finest tuxedos and red bow ties.

The Penguins moved amongst the mob with lavish trays of hors d'oeuvres. Each tray was adorned with a variety of delicacies fit for every taste and species in attendance. The dinner was fabulous. Music softly blended into the background atmosphere. The orchestra performed popular favorites as people partied and danced. Manny the seagull in human form performed a break dance to the delight of the crowd before his wedding dance with Minnie. The wedding dance was exquisite. Minnie and Manny embraced. They had come such a long way. Manny wondered where it was leading. "I have the love of my life, but somehow I perceive our happily ever after will be eventful." The story isn't over. Manny thought of his past life while embraced in Minnie's arms. Minnie dreamed of this moment and a tear of joy squeezed from the corner of one of her eyes as she held Manny even tighter and loved him ever more with each moment. Today they were joined forever. What was going to happen next? She knew they'd never again be put asunder. She knew they were mated for life. Minnie knew the future. She knew it all.

38

The festivities seemed to go on for days. Floyd gathered himself and made his way to a shady spot concealed in the clouds. He was preparing to go home. Manny saw him moving away from the festivities and followed him. "Floyd. Where ya goin?" Floyd smiled. "I'm getting myself ready to return to the twenty-first century and resume my life as a Manatee." Disappointed, Manny dropped his head between his shoulders. "Floyd, why can't you stay on with us? You've taught us so much and we need your wisdom now more than ever." A humble look and turned up lip expressed Floyd's humility. "Well," he paused, "You are now in a place where there's much greater wisdom to learn than I comprehend. You and Minnie have a specific mission, and "I" the great manatee," he smirked, "get to go back and see the results. I hope the cruel world we lived in will be changed because of you two. Not everything can go according to plan and I don't expect that, but it'll be a far better place to live because of what you and Minnie do here in this time. Generations to come will share your legacy. I want to be there Manny. I'll rejoice in your prosperity every day and be proud I've been a small part of the future to come as I see it made known." Manny mused. His lip was sort of quivering and his eyes were glassy. Manny felt like he was losing his best friend. "Floyd, will you answer one question for me?" "Sure," Floyd responded, "fire away."

"In the world we came from, the future, no one really cared to help anyone else do anything. We were more than a bit calloused to say the least, or maybe jaded is a better word. We never wanted to be involved in anyone else's "stuff" because we try to stay un-involved. Why are you so different? Is there anything in this for you?"

"Aha! Good question Manny. I'll take a stab at it and leave you with something to think about. This is short, simple and true. I once knew a mouse who told me this story. The mouse's name was Max. He adopted a house in the suburbs of Philly as his home. From early mouse-hood he understood his hosts weren't particularly fond of him. Max was always getting into their food and dragging it into his tiny hole in the wall apartment behind their refrigerator. Not much of a view, but it was safe. The resident family seemed to ignore his presence most of the time. One day he was scurrying across the floor and slid on some spilled milk. He fell head over heels into the whiskers of the cat, Jonah, who could have cared less about the presence of a mouse. At this time, however, Jonah was in a deep sleep. He jumped straight up, startled. Jonah landed in the lap of the little girl, Hanna, who was the eight year old daughter of his hosts, the Fladermauses. She was so surprised she dropped her soda and leapt to her feet. The table cloth was tucked into her belt and the entire contents of the table, breakfast for the family, flew all over the table and splattered on the floor and kitchen walls. Mrs. Fladermaus was startled and dropped the coffee pot which scalded the dog, Bofus. Bofus vaulted upward and bit Hanna's dad, Wolfgang, on the leg. Wolfgang screamed in agony and threw his juice at the dog. It missed and knocked over the bird cage where their happy cockatoo, Perry, almost had a heart attack. When the chain reaction finally ended, Wolfgang decided the family needed to get out of the house for breakfast. Max couldn't understand the language Wolfgang was "expressing" himself with. While having breakfast in a quiet and peaceful local restaurant, Wolfgang decided to stop at the local hardware store on the way home and purchase a mouse trap.

"This will take care of the problem once and for all," he muttered.

Later that morning, Max was grabbing a few crumbs when he heard the family car pull up. He ran back to his haven and waited and watched. Wolfgang entered through the kitchen door, and emptied the hardware bag on the counter. Looming before him was a MOUSETRAP! "OMG! What am I gonna do?" Max was mortified. When Wolfgang left the kitchen for a moment, Max ran over to Bofus and squealed in his high pitched voice. "Bofus! What am I going to do? Wolfgang bought a mousetrap and I think he wants to do me in. Bofus slobbered, raised his head with eyes half opened, and responded. "I could care less Max. You're a pain anyway. Now go away and let me get some sleep"

Max hung his head and started to walk away when he spotted Jonah. Max scampered directly to him as fast as his tiny legs would carry him. "Jonah! Jonah! I need your help. What am I gonna to do? Wolfgang purchased a mousetrap and plans to do me in." "Go away Max! Haven't you caused enough damage here today? I doubt anything will come of this anyway. He's a little unhappy that's all." "But, but Jonah," Max pleaded. "Go away mouse. Be gone!"

Max looked at Perry on his perch, high and away. "Perry, can you help me?" The bird turned his back and pooped all over the newspaper lying on the floor around him. The nasty mess narrowly missed Max. Max walked away dejected and rejected again.

Immediately, a new chain of events was set into motion. Wolfgang came back into the kitchen and set the mouse trap. Bofus, Jonah and Perry were all sleeping and never saw where he placed it. Wolfgang placed it on the open side of the refrigerator under the microwave stand. He crept out of the kitchen with a sly grin and went into his den to watch the football game.

Max came out and inspected the trap. Jonah had moved over to the microwave stand and thought he smelled something, probably the cheese in the trap. He began fishing with his paw under the microwave stand, as cats will do, and finally tapped something solid. Max ran under the stand and tried to kick the mousetrap away from Jonah's paw. He moved it to where Jonah had to stretch. Jonah batted the mousetrap and it flew out from under the microwave cart. The not so smart cat realized it was the mousetrap and tried to jump out of the way. It snapped with a LOUD bang and attached itself to the cat's tail. Jonah saw red! He hurdled so high he collided with the bird cage. This time poor Perry DID have a heart attack as his cage tumbled over on top of Bofus smashing into his backside and landing on his hind quarter with a painful thud. Wolfgang came running to the sound of the racket and tripped over the birdcage catapulting across the floor head long into the refrigerator. When the smoke cleared, Mrs. Fladermaus dialed 911.

Wolfgang was spirited off to the hospital in an ambulance with a splint on his neck, Bofus had to be taken to the vet and treated for a dislocated hind quarter, and Jonah went along to be treated for a broken tail. A day later poor Perry was buried in the back yard. He was literally scared to death.

"Now there is a moral to this story Manny. Listen to what I have to say. I was taught never to be indifferent as were Bofus, Jonah or Perry. They all ignored the warnings and pleas of Max and looked the other way. They were indifferent because they weren't involved. I learned long ago not be indifferent just because I perceive myself not to be involved. Indifference can lead to horrible consequences, as were described in Max's story. The only one hurt is the person who turns a blind eye. Sure, they may think they're avoiding harm's way, but sooner or later harm's way always finds its way to those who are indifferent."

Floyd smiled and peered deep into Manny's eyes. "This is why I choose to brighten every day with a smile and be a friend as a friend might be to me. What I do is who I am and I know I can make a difference in a world of indifference. In my reflections, I learn to believe in myself and recognize the world can be a better place to live if I try. All I need to do is transform my dream into reality and live as if it were real. Somehow, somewhere and sometime in my lifetime an opportunity may possibly come to pass. It came to me when Minnie was born. I spent my life preparing and living my dream.

Today my mission is complete. I made a difference when I was needed and now it's up to you. Move on Manny. Multiply and be happy." Floyd exuded satisfaction as he gripped his friend's hand firmly. "I need to get ready," Floyd continued. "Soon I'll be spirited off to the future. The ride's been adventurous nonetheless, and now it's time to be on my way."

As Floyd uttered his last sentence, he gradually became wrapped in a hazy white shade. Manny had more questions. What is this all about? What sort of "adventure" will he and Minnie travel and for what purpose? There was no time for questions. Before Manny could open his mouth Floyd became transparent. All at once and in a flash he was gone. The cloud was empty except for the presence of Manny. He felt sad and alone and although sounds of music and gaiety filled the air, Manny couldn't fully understand why this had to happen. He pondered a long time in silence before returning to the party. "I won't ever forget Floyd," he uttered under his breath. "I'll never forget my friend"

III. AND TIME STOOD STILL

39

As it was foretold, Floyd went home to the future. Manny returned to the party. Minnie wept when Manny gave her the news. In contemplative silence they looked out over the expanse and Minnie whispered quiet words of reflection. "Floyd's gone but for all time will remain in our hearts. Do you realize that Floyd isn't even born? I'll miss him but his friendship and insight will remain in me." Manny nodded, and with cloudy eyes they ventured into their new future from the past.

When the party was over Minnie and Manny were whisked to a land in Eden known as Paradises. There they found a small stream at the foot of picturesque mountains overlooking the landscape. A shoreline faced east from the mountains where they built a home and settled into their new lives. Even though both were human they sometimes continued to act like a fish and a bird. Manny wanted to build a nest but his new form wasn't compatible. Minnie had thoughts of finding something similar to the Crystal Cave underwater. After a few awkward attempts, adaption was gradually accomplished. Their diets were obviously different. Both of them needed to become accustomed to new diets as humans. Manny was okay with it because he ate a lot of picnic leftovers while roaming the beaches where humans hung out. Minnie was a full-fledged raw vegetable vegetarian and choked every time she smelled the aroma of anything cooked or fried, especially bacon. As time passed the transition was completed in spite of frequent challenges. Something was missing. An emptiness surfaced which neither could ignore. Prehistoric existence was primitive and uncomfortable at times. Paradises was a "nether-land" lacking modern conveniences such as smart phones, computers and Wi-Fi. However, this "place" wasn't exactly the Stone Age because they lived in a house, cooked on a stove and read by electric light. It was an "in-between" place created for them. Why?

Manny never fully understood the "so called" impending events which were supposed to ignite global change. It's easy to get lost in a forest and never see light streaming through its shaded canopy. Many times Manny had flown over life as a seagull and by no means perceived the joie de vivre of the world he was flying over. Minnie was a little more in tune. She envisioned life as art giving color and meaning to every dimension and experience. The planet was a painting to her. She didn't question her future and gratefully accepted her place on earth. Minnie recognized what was missing.

After a reasonable period of wedded bliss it was time to start a family. Minnie wondered if Manny was ready. Both maintained their original internal physiologies. She fantasized every day and night that they would be able to have children together. In the end Manny joined her dream and it came to pass.

40

In what appeared to be a vision Minnie wandered to the shoreline at sunrise and swam into the ocean. She was joined by Manny as they plunged into the warm placid surf. Minnie swam gracefully in a figure eight pattern as her eggs were made fertile by Manny who swam by her side. In their embrace the sky was filled with a warm floating mist. Their passion was endless as they swirled with the waves and sped through a forest of living coral. Time did not pass. The moment of their intimacy became a lifetime and two hearts beat as one in harmony with every living thing. In their reverie the mysteries of the ancient prophesies were revealed to their inmost sensitivities. With romantic conception consummated Minnie gathered the fertilized eggs into her bosom. Together, they were escorted by a covey of celestial doves and returned to Paradises.

Each day that passed Minnie became more festooned in supple radiance. Something extraordinary was transfiguring within her bosom. Manny cared for Minnie and remained steadfast by her side. What they had seen, where they had been and what was prepared was a miracle. A simple seagull and mythical mermaid were going to be parents. It was to be the greatest triumph for mankind thus far in the history of the new planet earth and it all began with a bird and a fish.

41

No more stories about pooping on Hoover Dam. No more stories about a little singing manatee or the Crystal Cave. No more days of hopeless meandering in a world where the sky was black with pollution and ice caps were melting away. No more corruption, wars, murders or madness to plague us. In all the years before only the darkest demons, evil and violence governed planet earth. The faint of heart were spared nothing. Agony and repression became a legacy of suffering. Even in the years of our greatest technological achievements nothing seemed to matter because the world was permanently tortured and blighted with dismal clouds of pending doom which never lifted before the next catastrophe unleashed.

Though Minnie and Manny had lived relatively simple and happy lives, they weren't far away from seeing Mother Terra's blight closing in on them. The world needed an awakening.

Manny and Minnie felt a profound veil was lifted for the enrichment of their spirits and a new beginning was near its inception. It was up to them to prepare the way. The dawn of a new age was close by and a birthday was around the next corner.

42

A monolithic shrine materialized before them. In front of it was a bright white staircase adorned in lilies. Behind it a brilliant illumination radiated into the firmament. The shrine itself was cast in pure gold. It hovered directly above the adorned structure over a spiral staircase. Its entrance way was supported with architecture of Doric, Ionic, Corinthian and Composite Columns. Each column was at least fifty feet tall. They were hewn in solid marble and ornamented with scroll work depicting flying seagulls upon their apex. Atop the columns a gigantic Romanesque archway was raised with images of mermaids symmetrically placed along its acme.   Behind the pillars loomed a triangular shaped

mammoth golden door so ornamented,
a facade of jeweled reflections gave rise
to every existing hue in the
immeasurable color continuum.

As Minnie and Manny moved closer,
they gradually rose to the foot of the
staircase. Each stride brought them
closer to the doorway. The great door
moved easily and on its own, beckoning
them to enter in. When they entered, it
closed behind them.
The day and hour of truth had arrived.
In front of Manny and Minnie a vast
chamber came into view. The floor was
made of pure deep blue turquoise tile
and checkered with white mother-of-
pearl tile for contrast. The white
mother-of-pearl represented the purity
of creation and its new born, and the
turquoise represented an expanse

where within anything is possible. In the geometric center of the room was a peculiar altar made of glass and precious stones. It was garland with an array of purple wild flowers randomly framing its outline. At the front of the altar were steps made of jade. Each one was smooth and decked with imbedded red and blue blazing sapphire borders. Minnie and Manny walked across the floor of the shrine and marveled at the stunning ornamentation on the inner walls and the giant frescos on the cathedral ceiling. The windows were all made of the finest stained glass which appeared to be carved from pure diamond stock, the facets of which reflected the crest of every rainbow to appear in the sky. As they arrived at the altar, an apparition manifested within a transparent globe. There in its midst was revealed a smiling manatee that looked a lot like Floyd. Minnie and Manny looked at each other and grinned. Manny raised one index finger and whispered to Minnie, "Is God a Manatee?"

Minnie was embarrassed and amused. From within the apparition a deep voice arose. "I am who I am. You see me as the gentlest creature on earth. You see me as a peace loving manatee and this is how I wish to be seen. I am here to bring the prophesies to fruition. "Minnie," he commanded, "ascend the steps of the altar and stand to the west." Minnie ascended the steps. "Kneel," he continued. Dutifully, she knelt and blended into the brilliance surrounding her. The altar "form-shifted" into a large transparent aquarium where she submerged her entire body. At that instant Manny was instructed to ascend the steps and sit on the edge to attend to his bride. Immediately the water roiled up and each of over a thousand fertilized eggs emerged from Minnie's bosom as tiny living beings.

In the background the Halleluiah Chorus filled the air. The walls swelled as gigantic organ pipes echoed a fantastic crescendo that instantly bathed them in a burst of energy from a vibration that exploded into stars and lit the night in every corner of the cosmos.
Minnie had given birth.

She was human which allowed her to mate with Manny who was human. Minnie produced over two-thousand babies. Each egg opened into an amnion of salt water within the altar. The organisms all bore attributes of mermaids, seagulls and humans. They resembled tadpoles with feet, and a human upper torso with miniature wings on their backs.

SO WHAT DO YOU GET WHEN YOU CROSS A SEAGULL WITH A MERMAID?

One of them rose from the water, and with its small wings, flew into Manny's arms. Manny gazed with loving approval into the luminous brown eyes of his first born. "This little lady I will name Angelica for the little girl who saved my life and made today possible." Manny's eyes widened as he turned his attention to Minnie, "Darling, you have a big job ahead of you. You can name the other one-thousand nine-hundred and ninety-nine!"

Minnie returned the look and softly whispered to Manny, "I will call all my children

"ANGELS."

43

Today Angels appear everywhere. They have guided and protected humans for centuries and formed great choruses to announce important celestial events. Angels know the heart of every individual. They are special creatures with a divine purpose.

Minnie and Manny became the parents of a new race. Love conquered all for a lovely mermaid and simple seagull.

Their lives and happiness are an example for all of us.

They taught us to look for beauty in everything, instead of condemning our differences.

44

With all his love Manny was transfixed by the aqua blue eyes of Minnie. Sunset was at her back and her reflection cast a shimmering silver shadow upon the deep. Her smile lit up the dusk as she returned his look. Together they breathed a quiet triumph in rhythm with the swell of the sea. Minnie and Manny stood serenely embraced overlooking the orange sky and the setting sun. The rolling tides reflected a panorama of dancing sunlight scattered randomly into the distance. A few gulls flew across their painting and the sounds of gentle waves washing upon the sand gave way to a warm sensation submerging their bare feet. A slight tropical breeze moved Minnie's hair as they breathed in the pure sweet aroma of an ocean at rest. The sky darkened, stars came out and every soul that ever lived became a light to the world.

They stood quietly enchanted by the vista of a cosmos at peace. All is quiet now. In the still of the night a voyage and a destination became one. Manny and Minnie are now home.

45

(21st Century)

Floyd laid down to rest for the last time in his long and significant life. His old eyes were weary. As a pastel veil of perpetual slumber dimmed his perception, he reflected for the last time upon his two friends from long ago. In his dream he envisioned an engraved stone tablet placed before him. On it was emblazoned a message from his wayfaring friends:

"When We Believed
We found love and came alive.
We awakened and there was light.
The sun shined upon us.
Stars lit the sky and music filled the air.
We moved to the music and danced.
We sang and became timeless.
Harmony transformed us.
Then we could fly.

It all began with love, a love from within.
When we shared our love with each other,
we believed
and the Angels inside were born."

On that day a new Hope was conceived
and Floyd slept in peace.

THE END

This is the story of how Angels
were born. They are always with us,
and if you believe they are with you too.

Epilogue

The truth? I concluded that a simple story was the most appropriate means for me to convey the imagination which led me to write. "Wings of Peace" was a unique adventure for me. I never knew how it would end when I began. It wrote itself as life is lived, ambling through time and reaching for greater meaning or spiritual enlightenment as I contemplated our place in the vast universe we inhabit. The story eventually made sense. My free-thinking fantasy was not linear or impeccably logical. It was born and grew from a positive freedom of expression which expanded as I released my mind into the furthest creative reaches of my own inner-realms and earned entry into a fantastic world of "other reality." Often times another reality will push my creative button. Then when I conjure expression from those remote depths, what follows becomes an unimpaired inspiration at its highest calling where anything can happen and usually does.
This is when I wrote "On Wings of Peace."

Jan Thomas Lust, 2012

Afterwords

DOVE AT MY FEET:

Sometimes the unexpected arrives long before we understand it. A seemingly inconspicuous event will bring important lessons into our lives. One of the things I've discovered is a concept called "Mindfulness." To me being mindful is an awareness of every detail in my multi-dimensional world. Things such as when I go out in the morning on the way to work and I see new flowers blooming. I see radiance and richness of color. How can there be no order to the universe when every morning around the world millions of flowers bloom all at the same time? Every landscape and design of nature is part of a delicate balance and harmony of nature's so called random patterns. I become mindful when I breathe in its nectar and open my heart to the universe. I see clearly all beauty in the most homely of nature's offerings and in innumerable unlikely places. In these most humble corners of creation I find serenity and balance. I also discover inward peace when I understand I'm spiritually in a little better condition than I was yesterday because I was able to see brighter colors in something today I didn't see yesterday. I can always decide to experience my joy and leave the rest. This brings genuine harmony to my spirit. I might easily go through life ignoring flocks of birds winging above, or graceful palms flexing with the will of the winds. I feel the rhythm of life giving sunshine to my eyes and music to my heart. Since I began practicing mindfulness I opened within to a new world I knew was there but eluded my perception. Those perceptions gradually changed and became focused as I began to feel a heightened wakefulness. Evaporating from my mind's eye was the stagnation that had previously mired my mind and undermined my ethereal development and tranquility. I'm no longer buried in the outer surface of basic survival. In reality my wits required much more than an outer appearance. I was in this frame of mind when the teacher arrived in the form of a dove.

I met her one morning while sitting on my patio reading a book enjoying a Florida sunrise. The sky was powdery blue and streaked with a pink reflection from a sun that leaped from the water and fused colors into a giant mural as it swirled into the eastern sky. In the stillness of that moment, I observed cool dewdrops clinging to the leaves of a small plantain tree on my patio. Only sounds of a rippling fountain and an occasional fish splashing in the water gave any sort of animation to a very surreal and peaceful time.

Suddenly, I heard a frantic wing flapping sound. The flapping was produced by a dove flying recklessly onto my patio without regard to the dangers that may be waiting for her. She landed on the fence. Swooping down on the dove was a blue jay. By the time the blue jay got to the fence she hopped down to the tiles on the patio and landed about a foot from my feet.

I was sitting in a rope hammock when rewarded by her visit. My feet dangled about three inches above the tiles as she walked around and explored her surroundings. The blue jay considered a moment and probably saw me sitting there. He decided not to come any closer and flew away. Miss Dove lingered a bit longer. In fact, for more than a week in the heat of summer she flew in every morning to greet me. She always landed on the patio picnic table, and occasionally jumped down to the tiles where she seemed content to sit near my feet.

If I gave any thought to this creature, I'd imagine she was trying to thank me for being there and saving her from the blue jay. In reality, I did nothing except observe. She "cooed" every morning until I joined her visit. I began to look forward to the soothing sounds of her cooing and our special bond. From her bright eyes and smooth feathery covering it appeared to me she was a young bird. There are some things we all know even when we're clueless. I knew she was a dove because she looked like a dove. I suspected she was a female, knew she was a female, but couldn't tell how I knew. I gave her a name, "Angel," because she came to me on Wings of Peace. The ritual continued daily. She thanked me by showing up, hanging out, and honoring me with her presence. After a while I think she decided I was thanked enough and flew away. I didn't know if she decided to go on with her life or if the blue jay finally got her. I wanted to remember that experience with a sort of reverence, therefore, I believed Angel was somewhere safe. Someday I hoped to see her again.

I especially remembered one particular morning during the "thank you" experience when Angel walked up on my foot and sat down. She looked directly into my eyes and smiled. I never saw a bird smile before but I was sure that's what she was doing. She relaxed to the point I thought she was about to take a nap on my foot. I always feel special when a creature that has no obligation to give me any sort of acknowledgement takes time to notice my presence. When an animal that normally fears man does not fear me, it tells me that whatever I'm projecting to that animal is most certainly not a projection of fear or intimidation.

I experienced similar occurrences in the past. Once, while hiking in the woods in Northern Pennsylvania, I came upon a small gathering of deer, all does and fawns. I stood still. One approached me cautiously as they all slowly gathered around me in a semi-circle. I extended my hand gradually, and one by one I felt their wet noses as they collected my scent. Another time I was hiking in the central West Virginia foothills when a single fawn burst from the brush and came up to me immediately. I reacted by offering my hand and the little fawn walked slowly under it. I petted his little forehead like a puppy for about five minutes.

By now I was beginning to feel Angel and I were becoming friends. Maybe our bond was stronger than I knew. Then she was gone.

It was the year of "nine-eleven." So much had happened. Current events were interfering with the spirituality I tried to maintain and grow toward. By the time Thanksgiving/Christmas season of 2001 came to pass I had forgotten the little things that mattered in the days of a very hot summer. One afternoon while stringing my Christmas lights on the patio, I came to a small sheltered garden where we raised orchids away from the direct sun. A miniature trellis covered by dense vines hung from a piece of driftwood that rested across the top under the balcony overhang. Not much light penetrated.

While stretching my lights through that area, I was surprised by the presence of a recently constructed bird nest. Roosting on the nest not more than two feet from my face was a young dove. About a week prior to her discovery, I kept hearing sounds of some sort of activity. I also heard the familiar sound of cooing. I never knew exactly what was going on in the orchid garden. Deep inside I hoped a nest was being built somewhere near. I wondered if my dove friend had returned. She was full grown now but looked so innocent and her eyes glowed with peace and contentment. She proudly sat on her nest. I held up a mirror once to see if there were any eggs. There were three. She permitted me to look, and as soon as I spotted them I moved away from the nest.

I didn't want to overstay my welcome. From then on I checked on her daily. She was always there. Once (shortly after Thanksgiving) she left the nest for a while. She probably needed a few things from the supermarket, or may have even gone to a local deli for a snack. I took the opportunity to hold the mirror up again and found the eggs intact. I knew she'd be back soon. Every night when I came out to turn on the Christmas lights I checked on her again. She was there as usual and radiant with the light of motherhood glowing from within her.

Now and then she hopped out of her nest to sit on one of the chairs, and subsequently glide to a patio tile near my feet. The day she walked up on my foot, sat down briefly and looked into my eyes was the day I knew she was my rescued dove from last summer. It was too much of a coincidence to happen twice, or with a different dove. I knew it was the same dove whose life was spared on that fateful day. Angel had returned to her adopted home to perpetuate her species. She had no fear of me whatsoever. I noticed another dove with her. He was larger and appeared occasionally but stayed mostly out of sight and reach. He must be the spouse. He regarded me whenever he saw me and cast his gaze to his lady who calmly blinked her pure brown eyes contentedly to return the look. From then on he behaved as though I was never there.

This year I attended a Christmas Eve service with friends. I enjoyed this time of year and looked forward to singing familiar Christmas Carols. When I returned home I went out on the patio to turn out the lights for the night. To my delight, on Christmas Eve at midnight I discovered her chicks had hatched. I heard their tiny peeps and witnessed mother dove comforting them. The miracle had happened. I stood back, not too close, and caught Angel's eye. She was as peaceful as I could ever dream to be in a lifetime.

What a perfect story! I'd like to leave it there, but time moves on whether we like it to or not. I believed this dove was going to teach me a lesson about life I needed to learn. I was so happy for the experience I shared it with all my friends and family.

About a week later I was taking down the Christmas lights when I learned in real life not all is happily ever after, or is it? I didn't hear anything in the nest. Mama dove was sitting on top of the trash can all puffed out and haggard looking. She seemed agitated and nervous. I didn't know what was causing it but she wasn't cooing. Her bright eyes were dry looking and appeared swollen. The silver cast of her down was dull and faded. I quickly found my mirror and looked in the nest. All three of her babies were still. For some unknown reason they had died. I left them in the nest for several days. Mother dove came back every day to mourn her loss. She kept returning to her nest to sit with them. There seemed to be no hope. Finally, she departed. I didn't know if I'd ever see her again. What a terrible depressing end to my perfect story.

Often times in the midst of a wrenching experience it's difficult to see we're on an endless path. Usually, most things happen for a reason, and nature's twists and turns twist and turn as they are supposed to whether we know it or not. Nothing ends where it ends, and nothing truly beautiful ever ends. Evil and ugliness are the only things that pass away sooner or later. Joy and love are forever. This is the lesson I was about to learn. There is no destination to a worthwhile expedition. A worthwhile trip is its own destination. Time is a dynamic concept. It doesn't stop. It always produces an aftermath. However, somewhere the story must conclude or the novel might run on forever as its own sequel! We, as humans, have invented a term called "closure." This allows us to end a chapter or story when resolution is achieved. I certainly felt no "closure" here. I didn't know the journey was continued. I thought it had reached its destination. Instead, I learned my precious dove contained tenacity beyond my understanding.

When I was sure Angel wasn't going to return, I cleaned out the nest and placed the lifeless chicks in a plastic bag and reverently disposed of their remains. I dismantled most of the nest and decided to move the orchids. I then placed a large storage bin in the area where once grew a garden. It wasn't the kind of place to raise baby birds anymore.

About a month or so later, while attending to morning chores, I looked up and there Angel sat atop the storage bin behind the trellis. She turned around and locked into my eyes with hers. A small twig was clasped in her bill. She was building another nest.

As time passed and her nest was rebuilt, Angel laid three eggs in her new nest, and thus her vigil began again. This time I held no expectations. I had a lot of hope, and I'm sure she held out no expectations either. Eventually the eggs hatched. For the next several weeks, I observed how she loved, nurtured and cared for her babies. Two of them survived. She permitted me to remove the one that did not. When she returned she appeared very approving to be in her nest with her living chicks. I sensed a comfort I couldn't explain. I kept up my observations from a distance and occasionally caught a glimpse of daddy dove in the fringes of their patio home. I observed as Angel raised her chicks into young adolescent avian(s), and was present to witness the day they stood on the edge of their nest resembling miniature doves preparing for a new adventure. She taught them to fly. In a few days, a joyous and bittersweet moment arrived. All I could do was watch as her family flew into the spring day sky, and say "thanks for the memory."

I learned a profound and moving lesson from Angel. I learned the meaning of becoming mindful. I recognized what it took to be the life I dreamed, and felt the change. In the end, life's simple wisdom was etched into my heart.

Be grateful for each day. Cherish it, and the gift of life we are given will also be our gift of happiness and everlasting peace, for how we live today becomes our memory of yesterday tomorrow.

All the healing we will ever need we will find within.

On Wings of Peace was a perfect title. I realized the Dove at my feet was the way I learned to see from my heart. In reality, I was the student at the Dove's feet. I learned then I wrote. The gift given to me is now yours. The message is summarized in the meaning of one word: HOPE.

Now, open your eyes take a deep breath, and let your Angel inside be free. No further words are necessary.

Made in the USA
Columbia, SC
30 August 2022

65891176R00163